Royalty Crowned Publishing

Raleigh, NC

www.royaltycrownedpub.com

ISBN: 978-0-692-13699-7

LCCN Library Congress: 2021913170

Copyright: 1-8634021671

Cover Design: Tori Mckoy

Cover Photo: Tori Mckoy

Edited By: Carla Dean

This book is dedicated to all the women who have been betrayed by someone they loved. Special dedication to the women who raised me RIP Mommy and Nana.

First of all, I want to give praises to the most high for being a constant factor in my life and blessing me with the talent to constantly create content.

To my three KINGS: Shaimek, Shacory and Sharhon Williams, Mommy will forever teach y'all perseverance, consistency, survival, strength, and most of all resilience. I will not let y'all subject yourselves to be a product of your environment but rise to breaking generational transfer.

To my Princess in Heaven Shaquoia Elizabeth Cherraine Williams I miss you baby.

Shaimek and Jayla thanks for giving me the greatest gift of all my granddaughter Samaya Shaquoia Williams aka Tootie. Mi Mi loves you baby girl.

To my mother, Angela Melvin and Nana, Virginia Edwards. SIP my beautiful angels. I didn't know what life was going to be without y'all but I'm pushing through it. Even when I get weak and want to give up, the mere thought of y'all keep me going. Y'all are my light when life seems dark.

To the only father I know, Charles Edwards, SIP Grandad I thank God for you and the hand you had in raising me. You got to walk me down the aisle, you took me to my first day of school, you were there when I graduated, and for so much more. You became the father figure I didn't have and I thank you for showing me what a hard-working man looks like.

To my father, Alexander McEachin, SIP Father. I thank God for the time I got to spend with you and how I was able to close that hurtful chapter in my life. Even though we didn't have much of a relationship, you took part in creating me and I thank you for life itself.

To my Present and Future Flint "Raheem" Reaves, you become my sunshine on a cloudy day. You taught me to depend on God and not people. You showed me genuine love and support. You turned my broken past into a pool of healing. I'm forever grateful for the impact you have on me and my sons life. May God continue to bless our union. Let's Do this #TeamReavesToBe

To my bonus children, Sydney and Flint Reaves I love you both as my own. I can't wait to create memories with y'all and become a beautiful blended family.

To my besties, Tara Miller, Erica Mitchell, Michelle McCullough and Shon Juan, I love y'all to infinity and beyond. No matter what challenges our friendships have faced y'all never turned y'all backs on me. We never crossed each other to the point of no return. Real friendships real women. Y'all all have been there for me in different ways and supported me one way or another. I thank God for giving me such a great set of women in my circle.

To my siblings Danielle Melvin, Buddy "Jay" Melvin, Deon "KK" Melvin, Derrick Freeman and Sean McEachin, I thank for y'all being a part of my life. Please continue to live out your dreams and continue being great parents to my nieces and nephews. Love you all more than words can expressed.

To My Uncle Mickey and Aunt Pam, I thank God that we still have y'all in our lives. Please live life to the fullest as I know Nana would want y'all to do so just as she did. Y'all have become the head of the family. I'm grateful for you both.

To all my cousins, I love y'all and just know rather near or far there is no love lost. We are and always will be family.

To the rest of my family and friends I love you all and I thank y'all for the continuous support and love.

Shoutout to my Brooklyn, Chapel Hill, and Raleigh Famm I came to North Carolina young but I will never forget where I came from. I definitely won't forget the grind and struggle that I was bred and fed.

I want to thank my photographer Tori McKoy you always capture my vision and body it. Carla Dean my editor thanks for everything you've done to help me push this project. Keith Williams, for my graphics and stepping in last minute and giving me a fire cover.

Thanks to all of you who have supported and brought my products throughout the years. I appreciate the continued love and support. I'm not done yet.

After The Betrayal

By Tamika Melvin

Deja Vu

Chapter 1

S itting deep in thought, Endy stared out the open window at the cardinal perched in a tree as she inhaled the fresh southern air, reflecting on what her life had become. The last three months had been traumatic, but she knew it was time for her to leave North Carolina and face reality.

When Endy set Jasean's car ablaze, she called her aunt and told her what happened. After a lengthy scolding, Aunt Linda invited her niece to come to Raleigh North Carolina so she could get away from everything for a while and clear her head. Knowing she might do something she would later regret if she stayed in New York, Endy quickly accepted her aunt's offer.

Her cousin, Rocko, and best friend, Niema, had moved to Raleigh soon after the ordeal; however, Endy hadn't seen or spoken to either of them during the entire three months she had been there. In fact, ever since she caught her husband screwing that whore YaYa in Miami three months ago, she hadn't talked to anyone but her mother, Tanya, and her cousin, Chynna.

As requested, Endy's mother and cousin had flown down south to reunite Endy with her daughter, Patience. During the short time they were there, the two women begged Endy—who was now pregnant with her second child—to come home. But, at the time, Endy wasn't ready to face what was waiting for her back in the Big Apple. To add salt to the injury, Endy found out YaYa had given birth to a baby boy three days prior and named him Jasean Newman Jr., which meant Jasean had been cheating for months.

If it weren't for Jasean going on trial for the extortion and money laundering charges he caught the year prior, she would have stayed right there with her aunt. The detectives reached out to Endy to let her know Jasean exonerated her from any connection with the charges. Now Endy had to salvage what she could of the business she had worked so hard to build.

The shuffling of Aunt Linda's house slippers broke Endy from her deep thinking.

"Hey, sugar plum. How you doing?"

"I'm good, Auntie. Just not ready to go back to New York," Endy said as she rubbed her belly and sighed.

"Well, baby, you can't run forever. You have to face this shit head-on, but don't you worry. Jasean and that tramp will get what's coming to them soon enough. God will handle everything; I promise. You just focus on getting things back on track concerning your business and home life. If not for you, do it for your babies. You've worked too hard to lose it all."

Linda walked over and gently rubbed Endy's belly, feeling nothing but sadness for her great-niece.

"I don't even know where to start. Then, on top of everything, he might have to do some time in prison. Meanwhile, I'll be out here raising two kids alone while trying to get my business back straight. Let's not forget the other baby he has now. I'm just so confused. Why is all this happening?" Endy rhetorically asked. She placed her palms against her forehead in exasperation while thinking about what she would have to deal with on her own.

"God won't put more on you than you can bear. You can't let the devil win, Endyia. You're a fighter, honey; you have Hinton blood running through your veins. Get up and go get your life back!" Linda cheered.

Endy giggled. "You're right, Auntie, but I can't get over the fact he has a baby with that chick. I guess it explains why she kept coming for me. I feel so stupid."

Endy shook her head as she recalled the not-so-great encounters with YaYa.

"Baby, she envied you from day one. Everything I've heard about this mess proves she was jealous of you. There's one thing I want you to do for me, though."

"What's that, Aunt Linda?"

"Make amends with Rocko and Niema. They love you, Endyia. Niema had a lot going on, so I believe her if she said she really didn't know. Besides, you haven't even seen your godson, Nasim, and he's a month old already."

"I know, Auntie. I'm just hurt because I wish she would have warned me as soon as she heard something. My life will never be the same. Never."

Feeling the tears pool in her eyes, Endy blinked them back forcibly–she was tired of crying.

"It will get better, baby. I promise you, but you have to face this so you can move past it. You can't run from this one, Endyia. You can't."

Endy knew her aunt was right, which is why she knew it was time to return to New York.

"Well, I better go get my things together. I will need to head to the airport soon, and Cousin Thee is on her way to take me."

Endy gave her face a quick pat and started up the stairs. About halfway to the top, a knock at the door stopped her.

"I got it, baby," Linda assured her, rushing to the door as Endy continued to her room.

AFTER THE BETRAYAL

Linda swung open the door, and there stood Niema holding Nasim in her arms.

"Hi, sweetie. I almost thought you weren't coming!" Linda exclaimed as she kissed Niema on the cheek and quickly took the baby from her.

"Sorry I'm late, Aunt Linda. I had so much to do this morning. Thanks for letting me know she was leaving, though. I didn't handle this situation the best way, and I want to let her know I love her. I was stuck in the middle of two people I love. I felt like my cousin was just talking when she told me that he tried to holla at her. I seriously didn't think she was telling the truth," Niema explained.

"Baby, I think you should express all that to Endyia so y'all can put this mess to rest."

"You're right, Aunt Linda. I might as well face the music. It's been way too long."

Niema sucked in a deep breath, exhaled slowly, and prepared herself to face whatever Endy had to say. After slowly ascending the stairs, she knocked lightly on the bedroom door.

"Come in!" Endy called out, thinking it was her cousin Thee.

When she caught sight of Niema standing in the doorway, she rolled her eyes and grumbled under her breath. She was certain her aunt had arranged this ambush.

"What's up, Ny?" Endy dryly greeted while shoving some clothes in her suitcase.

"Hey, Endy. Aww! You are so cute with your baby bump!" Niema said, trying to sound cheerful despite her voice trembling.

Endy shot her a mean look and continued to pack her things. Niema knew she took a chance popping up on her like that, but she missed her best friend. She was nervous as hell but needed Endy to know she had no idea that her cousin and Jasean were messing around until it was too late.

"Look, I know you don't want to see me right now," Niema said. "But don't you think we owe it to ourselves to see if our friendship is worth saving? Endy, I swear I didn't know what to do. It had already happened."

Endy shot her an evil look. Niema could see the anger and pain in Endy's tear-filled eyes, and it hurt her to know she may have contributed to that.

"Ny, you don't get it, do you? You could have given me a warning or something, but you chose not to. And now, my whole life has changed! I'm about to be a single mother, and my husband have a third child with your cousin, which makes that child your cousin. This shit is fucking crazy!" Endy ranted, pacing back and forth.

"I know, Endy, but please believe me when I say I had no idea. YaYa moved to Upper East Manhattan, so I thought maybe she found some old-ass guy to sponsor her lifestyle. Never did I think she was dealing with Jasean, especially on that level. When she told me that she could have Jasean if she wanted to, I thought the hoe was just talking!"

"I know, Niema, but it hurts to know he would do this with your family. He knew I was bound to find out," Endy groaned.

"Please know if I see that trick, it's over for her ass on sight. I love you, and for her to hurt you like this kills me. I never knew her jealousy would drive her to do something as cruel as this, Endy. I swear I never thought she would take it this far. She knows how much I love you and my goddaughter. It hurts me that you haven't seen your godson." Niema could no longer hold back her tears.

"Don't cry, Ny," Endy said, taking a step closer to her. "I know you didn't know every-thing that took place. I just wish you would've given me a clue that she even mentioned something about her and Jay. At least I could've kept my eyes open, but you know what? I got this."

Endy shook the negative thoughts out of her head as she closed the distance be-tween them and hugged Niema, who sobbed harder. Endy cried, too.

"Ny, I'm sorry I took my frustration out on you. I was just so angry. I feel like I'm trapped in a nightmare," Endy expressed to her.

Hugging each other tightly, they knew their friendship was still solid.

AFTER THE BETRAYAL

"Well, let me get my ass back to New York so I can stop running and deal with this shit," Endy sighed.

"E, never question my loyalty to you. When you hurt, I hurt. I love you and Patience so much. Please know that."

The two women hugged it out, then went downstairs so Endy could head to the airport.

BACK 2 LIFE, BACK 2 REALITY

Chapter 2

Endy, Niema, Thee, and Aunt Linda rode to Raleigh-Durham International Airport in silence.

Apprehensive about Endy going home, Aunt Linda finally spoke. "Baby, I'm going to miss you. I enjoyed you staying with me and keeping me company."

"I know, Aunt Linda, but you never know, I might make that move next!"

"Good. I would be happy. Then maybe the rest of them will come, too," she replied.

"Now, y'all know Lu Lu is not coming down here!" Thee said, referring to Endy's grandmother.

"She sure ain't coming down South," Niema chimed in, laughing.

"Yeah, she especially is not leaving Pablo's ass behind. That's her Boo Bear," Aunt Linda added.

"Y'all leave my nana alone. She loves her man, but she loves New York more." Endy burst into laughter.

Fifteen minutes later, they arrived at the airport.

"I'm gon' miss your ol' crazy self," Aunt Linda told Endy.

AFTER THE BETRAYAL

"I'm gon' miss you, too, Auntie."

After getting Endy's luggage from out of the trunk, they all headed inside so Endy could check her bag.

"Keep in touch. And you know if you need to get away, my door is always open," Niema said lovingly.

"I know. Don't be surprised if my ass moves down south with y'all," Endy replied with a chuckle.

"That might not be a bad idea. You may need a new start," Aunt Linda commented, her tone serious.

"I know, Auntie. Let me handle my business first, and we will see."

Endy hugged and kissed her godson, feeling regretful for not seeing him during her stay in Raleigh. She then kissed Nasim on his forehead, while Niema kissed Patience on the cheek.

Linda smiled as she looked at them. She knew the two women had overcome a lot in the past year, but it was clear to see they still loved each other very much.

"Okay, y'all, they just announced my flight."

Endy grabbed Patience by the hand so they could head toward the growing line to board the airplane.

"I love you, Sugar Plum. Be safe," Linda told her niece before Endy disappeared into the crowd of people.

Once Endy boarded her flight, she immediately started thinking about what she would have to face when she got back to New York.

"God, please be with me," she whispered, then gently kissed Patience on her fore-head.

◆ ❤ ◆ RoyaltyCrowned ◆ ❤ ◆

When Endy arrived at LaGuardia Airport, Chynna was there to pick her up.

"What's up, cuzzo? I missed you so much." She rushed to Endy for a hug.

"I missed y'all, too, but I would be lying if I said I'm happy to be back in New York," Endy replied while handing a sleeping Patience to her cousin.

"I know, but before you know it, this will all be over. What I need you to do is relax and handle your business. I promise I'll be here for you every step of the way," Chynna assured her.

"How's everybody doing?" Endy asked.

"I'm not gon' lie. Shit's been hectic, but no worries. Your concern right now should be bringing a healthy baby into the world. Okay?" Chynna told her as they exited the airport after retrieving Endy's suitcase from the baggage carousel.

Endy sat in silence during the entire ride home, overthinking how she would live without Jasean. Always well prepared to handle most situations, this shit had blindsided her. She knew YaYa was jealous of her and Niema's relationship, but she never thought this would be the outcome—not in a million years.

Thirty minutes later, they finally arrived at her house. As Endy stepped out of the car, a knot grew in her stomach. She tried hard to ignore it as she got Patience out of the backseat and headed towards the house. But, with each step, Endy became increasingly uneasy. She had to figure out her next move—and fast.

"You sure you want to stay here?" Chynna asked while opening the door.

"I'm good, Chynna, for real. That clown gon' regret ever crossing me, and that's a promise," Endy said through gritted teeth as she slammed the door behind her after getting her daughter inside.

"Have you seen the baby?" Chynna asked.

"No, and I don't want to either. So, don't ask me stupid-ass questions!"

9

AFTER THE BETRAYAL

"Okay, cuz, I got you. Remember, I'm on your side. I was just wondering if you saw pictures or anything on Facebook or Instagram?"

"No. YaYa's punk-ass blocked me right after all that went down because she knew I was gon' call that ass out."

"Look, I need you to calm down until you have the baby. After that, we can turn up on that chick."

"Chy, I'm not gon' lie. This shit hurts like hell. I don't even know how I should feel anymore. A part of me still loves him deeply, but on the other hand, I despise the bastard. I've been praying for God to take this hurt away, but I know it's only been three and a half months. So, I need to give myself time." Endy lowered her head, feeling somber.

Ding-dong! Ding-dong! Ding-dong!

"Who the hell is ringing my doorbell like that?"

"I forgot to tell you. I told the cousins to come by...just the girls, though."

"Chynna..."

"I know, E, but you need your family around. We're not leaving you in this damn house alone."

"I guess I have no freaking choice."

"Hell no, you don't," Chynna said, laughing as she raced to open the door.

"Hi, cousin!" Asia shouted as she rushed past Chynna to get to Endy.

"Well, damn! Hello to you, too, Asia. Hi, my beautiful cousins." Chynna giggled as she hugged Egypt and Karishma.

"Girl, you know Asia and Endy have a love-hate relationship," Egypt stated, laughing.

"I'm so glad you're home, Endy. I've been holding down the shop, but I so missed you being here," Karishma told her.

"I know Rizzy. Despite everything, I missed my family too," Endy admitted.

"Cuz, I know you feel alone in this shit, but we got your back in whatever decisions you make," Egypt said supportively.

"I know, and I thank y'all for being here for me."

"Well, if you ask my opinion, I think you need to divorce his ass—get alimony and child support. He needs to pay for hurting you like this, Endy. I told y'all we can't trust these dudes out here. They're all dogs. You can't let him get away with this bullshit," Asia interjected.

"Would you mind your damn business?" Chynna snapped. "She doesn't need to hear all that right now."

"Ain't nobody talking to you, Chynna. That jerk needs to be dealt with for what he did to her. Y'all just can't blame YaYa. But, trust, her ass is gon' get what's coming to her, too," Asia added.

"Come on, y'all," Endy said, trying to calm the women down. "I'm not taking this shit rolling over, believe that. But, tonight, I want to enjoy this time with my family."

"You're right. I apologize. We shouldn't even be discussing this mess right now. We're here to support you, and that's what we're going to do," Asia said, shooting daggers with her eyes at Chynna.

"Thanks, cousin. Chynna, you good?" Endy asked.

"I'm good...and I'm sorry, Asia. We need to be pulling together instead of going at each other's necks," Chynna said and hugged her cousin.

"I just don't like seeing my people hurt," Asia expressed. "I know how these dudes move. Endy's a good person, and she doesn't deserve this shit, man!"

"Asia, you crying? I can't believe the big bad wolf is crying!" Egypt exclaimed, then started laughing.

Asia stopped crying and broke into laughter, too, at Egypt's remark.

"Y'all, for real, don't worry about me. I promise y'all that once I drop this little one, shit is gon' change," Endy assured them.

AFTER THE BETRAYAL

"My only concern is that you're okay, but I promise you that YaYa is going to get it on sight. No questions asked," Karishma blurted out.

"Let me find out Rizzy ready to turn up," Asia said and high-fived Egypt.

"I know, right?" Endy laughed.

"Yeah, I'm ready to kick somebody's ass, but we gon' let it go for now," Karishma told Endy.

"Thanks, guys. Well, let's put on some music and play some cards. I know tomorrow I will have to face the music, so let me have some fun tonight," Endy pleaded.

The girls did what she asked, and it was like old times again. They spent the night dancing, singing, and enjoying each other. They were glad Endy was back from North Carolina, and Endy finally felt glad to be back home with family.

◆ ❤ ◆ RoyaltyCrowned ◆ ❤ ◆

The following day when Endy woke up, she tried to mentally prepare herself to see Jasean for the first time in three months.

"How you feeling, babe?" Chynna asked Endy after finding her staring blankly at her reflection in the mirror.

"I feel like I'm having a nightmare that I can't wake up from," Endy replied with a lost look in her eyes.

"Well, you're going to have to face him sooner or later, so you might as well get it over with."

Chynna walked up behind her and rubbed her shoulder.

"Yeah, I know, but what do I say to him when I get there?"

"Say whatever you feel, Endy. You have a right to be as mean and vulgar as you want.

After everything you have endured, he can't think this would be a pleasant visit. Believe me, he's just going to be happy to see you and Patience," Chynna reassured her.

"I guess you're right," Endy agreed, then hugged Chynna and wiped away her tears before leaving to head to Clinton Correctional.

After the drive to the airport, Endy, with Patience attached to her hip, Chynna, and their mutual best friend, Ari, boarded Jasean's Uncle Jack private plane. They accompanied Endy for moral support. The flight to the prison was short and quiet, but the whole time all Endy could think about was how she was going to feel once she and Jasean were face-to-face.

♦ ♥ ♦ RoyaltyCrowned ♦ ♥ ♦

"Jasean Newman!" the guard yelled.

Jasean's palms were sweating, and his stomach was in knots as he made his way to the visiting area. He didn't know what Endy was going to say when she saw him. All he knew was he wanted to see her and his baby girl. He was ready to pour his heart out and give her all the answers she wanted.

As she walked over to him with Patience in tow, his stomach fluttered with butterflies. When she finally reached the table, he stood to hug her, but she quickly handed him Patience and sat down to avoid having physical contact with him.

"Hi, baby. You're glowing so much," Jasean said, attempting to break the ice.

Not knowing what else to say, he fell silent.

"Thanks, Jay," Endy finally responded.

"No, thank you for coming. I know I'm probably the last person you want to see, and--"

"You got that shit right," Endy said, cutting him off. "I'm only here to discuss business, and so Patience can see you. She will be a year old soon and misses you."

"Dada...Dada..." Patience babbled.

"Aww Daddy missed you so much, princess," Jasean said, planting kisses all over his baby girl's face.

Endy couldn't help but notice how good Jasean looked. Even in the orange jumpsuit, he was sexy to her. She wanted him in the worse way, especially since the pregnancy had her hormones going wild.

"You look so gorgeous, babe," Jasean said as he looked Endy up and down.

She shifted in her seat while trying to hide the blush creeping on her face.

"Thanks, Jay."

"I miss y'all so much, Ma. I want you to know I'm going to do everything I can to make this right," Jasean said.

He extended his arm over the table to grab her hand, but she quickly snatched it back out of his reach.

"I'm going to get a soda. Do you want anything?"

"Nah, sexy. I'm good."

Endy rolled her eyes and walked off in the direction of the vending machines. She hoped eating a snack would calm the baby doing somersaults in her belly. Meanwhile, Patience planted kisses all over her daddy's face. He was enjoying every minute of it.

"You shouldn't be eating all that salt," Jasean chided when Endy returned.

He watched as she continued stuffing the barbeque-flavored Wise potato chips in her mouth.

"Dude, you worried about chips right now?" she said with sarcasm, then chuckled and shook her head.

"Well, you won't talk to me. I'm just trying to make conversation."

"Okay, you want to talk? Let's talk," Endy snapped as she slammed her can of orange Sunkist soda down on the table.

"E, I'm not trying to argue with you. I want us to get past this bullshit, that's all."

"Motherfucker, did you really just say that? Did you just say you want us to get past this bullshit when this bullshit is all your fault?"

"E, calm down. I'm just saying I want us to get over this situation. I messed up, but I want you to know that you and the kids are the most important people in my life," Jasean said in a soft voice full of regret.

"Don't you tell me to calm down! I could slap the shit out of you right now, but I'm not trying to go to jail today. Your best bet is to enjoy your time with your daughter and leave that subject alone. I didn't go off and have a baby with someone else. You did, asshole!"

"E, please...I love y'all and don't want to lose my family over this," Jasean pleaded.

"Jay, let's stop talking about this bullshit. I'm strictly here for Patience and business. All that other shit is irrelevant right now."

"Okay, well, I put everything in your name, and I cut all ties with it so you won't get caught up in anything I got going on. You just do what you need to do for you and the kids. I got me covered," Jasean told her.

"Yeah, I will do everything I can to make sure my children are good...best believe that."

A FRIEND OF MINE

Chapter 3

I t was summertime, and Endy had been home for about a month. During this time, she stayed busy with doctor's appointments, business meetings, handling store inventory, and simply doing mom things—all this while also traveling back and forth down South.

"What's going on? Where's Endy?" Chynna asked as she and her mother, Lisa, strolled into the boutique.

"I don't know. She said she had to make a run and would be right back," Karishma replied.

"It's not like Endy not to check in with anybody. Something isn't right. I feel it. Has she been back to see Jay?" Lisa inquired.

"Well, I know she went to North Carolina last week," Karishma told them. "She said it was about an apartment, but she never mentioned it again."

Just then, the door to the boutique opened, and Endy's mother, Tanya, entered.

"Hi, y'all! What brings y'all here?" Tanya said, greeting her niece and sister.

"We were seeing if we could catch Endy, but she isn't here...again. Did you know she went to North Carolina about an apartment last week?" Chynna asked her aunt.

"No, but Aunt Linda called me to make sure everything was okay. She said Endy went down there, stayed the night, and was gone by morning," Tanya shared.

"Well, I got to get back to Queens to get Enrique from Reeko mother's house. When Endy comes back, let her know we stopped by," Chynna said before she and her mother left.

Once they were gone, Tanya whispered, "Rizzy, you didn't say anything else about the trip to North Carolina, did you?"

"No, Auntie, I didn't. Endy did say if any of the family came looking for her, I should tell them that she went to look at an apartment and that she's been busy getting things back in order," Karishma answered.

"Okay, well, when she does get here, tell her to call me. She's nine months pregnant and due any day now. So, she needs to chill with all this moving around. Oh, and let her know I'm going by Evelyn's house to pick up Patience," Tanya added, then hurriedly picked up her purse and headed out the door.

"Hold up!" Endy said as she appeared from the back area of the boutique.

Startled, Tanya shrieked, "You were hiding from us!"

"No, Ma, not you. I saw Aunt Lisa and Chynna on the camera, so I stayed in the back until they left. I'm tired of everyone being all in my business and questioning me about Jasean having a baby with YaYa. I just didn't feel like being bothered."

"Well, I'm going to get my granddaughter. I miss her, and so does your nana. You really need to get some rest," Tanya told her daughter, then turned to Karishma and said, "And don't you lie to me again."

"Ma, that's my fault. Don't blame Rizzy. As for me getting some rest, I just need to finish this paperwork, and I'll be done for the day. Rizzy already said she would lock up," Endy informed her mother.

AFTER THE BETRAYAL

"Great! I will check on you later," Tanya said as she left the store.

When the coast was clear, Endy immediately asked Karishma, "You didn't tell her anything, did you, Rizzy?"

"No, Endyia. I told you I got you. I promise," Karishma reassured her.

"Cool. Well, once I finish this paperwork, I'm gon' head on home."

◆ ❤ ◆ RoyaltyCrowned ◆ ❤ ◆

As Endy drove home, she felt a slight cramp, but she didn't say anything because she didn't want to alarm Karishma. Once she dropped her off, she went straight home. She felt a slight pain again, so she texted Chynna and told her to meet her at her house as soon as possible. She awkwardly waddled up the stairs of her house to pack a bag, and as soon as she reached for her final item, her water broke.

"Damn it! No!" she panicked.

Abandoning her packing efforts, Endy quickly went to the closet to retrieve her hospital bag. As she made her way back to the bed, she started to feel lightheaded and sat down on the edge of her mattress. She picked up her phone to text Chynna again, but she passed out before she could press the send button.

Twenty minutes later, when Chynna got there, she noticed the door unlocked and ajar. She called out to Endy, but there was no response. Chynna rushed up the stairs to the bedroom to find Endy unconsciously sprawled on the bed. Grabbing Endy's phone from her hand, she immediately called 911.

"I need an ambulance! My cousin is nine months pregnant, and she's passed out and not responding! Please hurry!"

About thirty minutes later, they arrived at New York Methodist Hospital. Most of Endy's close ones were already there. The family was alarmed by all the tubes running in and through her. EMS workers asked the family to stay behind in the waiting room while they rushed Endy through the doors to begin working on her.

"God, please don't let anything happen to my baby girl!" Tanya cried, dropping to her knees.

"It's going to be okay, Auntie. We have to be strong right now," Chynna said, attempting to comfort her.

After two hours of waiting, a doctor finally approached the family.

"Well, the baby is here, and he's healthy as an ox. As for Ms. Newman, we had to do an emergency C-section, but she is doing fine. She passed out due to high blood pressure, dehydration, and exhaustion, but she got here just in time. You all should be able to see her very soon."

"Wait...did you say he? Don't you mean she?" Lisa asked.

"No, that was our little mix-up. She had a baby boy," Dr. Blake smiled, knowing Endy wanted a boy all along.

"Oh my God, Endy must be so happy! Wow, another boy in the family!" Chynna sang.

Tanya raced from the back with tear-filled eyes and a smile on her face.

"It's a boy, y'all! The ultrasound was wrong!" she cheered as she gave her husband a huge hug.

"When can we see her?" Karishma asked.

"We should be able to in a few. The doctor said he would call us back after they get them cleaned up."

Ring! Ring! Ring!

"It's Jasean," Chynna said, looking down at Endy's phone that she had been holding ever since she called for the paramedics. "Should I answer it?"

"Yeah, you might as well. It's still his baby," Luella, their grandmother, told her.

Tanya didn't look too fond of Luella's response, but she knew she was right.

"Hi, Jay. This is Chynna. Your wife just had the baby."

"Wait, what? How long ago? Damn, I been trying to call for the last two hours."

"Well, she had some complications, but she and the baby are fine. We're waiting to go to the back now."

"Does she look like Patience?"

"Auntie said he looks just like you."

"Wait, he? What you talking about? I thought they said it was a girl?"

"Well, the doctors made a boo-boo. Y'all have a nine-pound, two-ounce baby boy!" Chynna said, and the phone went silent. "Jay? Are you there?"

"Yeah, man. I can't take this shit. I want to see my baby!" he hollered through the phone.

"Well, we're going to take pictures and can send them to you. Just keep your head up and focus on getting home to your family. Jay, I love you, but you got a lot of fixing to do when you come home," Chynna warned him.

"I know. Tell the family I said hello, and let my wife know I love her and wish I was there. Yo, is Ma Dukes there?" Jasean asked.

"Nah, but she should be here shortly. She said she and Marilyn were on their way."

"Newman family?" a nurse yelled.

"Jay, I got to go. We're about to go back and see the baby, but I will be sure to tell everyone what you said. Oh yeah, and congratulations."

"Babe, that was Nana on the phone. She said Endy had the baby, and guess what?" Niema shouted to Rocko.

"What?" he replied, his face screwed up.

"She had a boy instead of a girl!" Niema announced.

"Wait, what? Oh, shit, yo! That's crazy. I know she's happy as hell!"

Rocko jumped up from the recliner where he was perched playing NBA 2K15 on the PS4.

"Bae, let's catch a flight to New York for about a week. We can get Aunt Linda and Nana together for a little bit," Niema suggested.

"I don't know, babe. I love my cousin and all, but that drama is still going on. I'm not feeling that shit," Rocko replied.

"Well, you can stay here in Raleigh, but Nasim and I are going to New York. See you in a week," Niema said as she whisked upstairs to pack.

"I might as well go and get my baby from her grandmother house while I'm up there, too," he whispered to himself while shaking his head, knowing damn well he couldn't tell Niema no.

"Ayo, bae, I'm in! Damn!"

"I know. That's why I already booked the tickets!" she yelled from upstairs.

Ring, ring, ring!

Niema's phone rang, but not recognizing the number, she ignored it. Yet, the more she ignored it, the more it kept ringing. So, she finally picked up.

"Hello?"

"So, you can't call to check on your new baby cousin? But I bet you're going to let Lil' Roc see Endy's baby."

Niema was shocked to hear YaYa's voice on the other end. When Rocko appeared into view, she couldn't utter a word.

"What's the matter? Who's on the phone?" Rocko asked.

"YaYa!" she replied in shock.

AFTER THE BETRAYAL

"Yo, what the fuck she wants?"

YaYa hung up as soon as she heard Rocko yelling in the background.

"She hung up. I don't know how she got my number... It had to be Aunt Sally."

"Well, she better not start no bullshit."

"Baby, I swear to you we haven't spoken since all that went down back in February."

"I know that, babe. I'm not blaming you. I'm just aggravated as hell with all this drama happening. I hate things had to go down like that. It's like shit ain't been the same with the family. Everybody's doing their own thing!"

"Well, babe, maybe when we get up there, we can plan something for all the family to come together. But now that she called, I need to get up there as quick as possible."

"Why did she call? What did she say?" Rocko asked.

"She commented on how I haven't come to see her baby yet and that I'm probably going to go see Endy's baby with Lil' Roc."

"You mean to tell me you didn't say nothing, and she already knows Endy had the baby? Somebody is being shady as fuck, and I'm going to find out who. Yeah, let's head up North. We don't need nobody else going to jail," Rocko said, gathering the baby's stuff while Niema called Aunt Linda.

By morning, they were in New York and heading to Luella's house. They needed to make sure YaYa didn't try any funny mess with Endy or the new baby.

♦ ❤ ♦ RoyaltyCrowned ♦ ❤ ♦

"Thanks for coming to visit me. These bitches really think they're about to have their babies in peace while we suffer? Not if I have anything to do with it!" Taiya Rocko baby mother told YaYa and Lynasia.

Lynasia was J.J. baby's mother, who was sitting alongside YaYa on a prison visit.

"I'm tired of all of them—my cousin Niema, Endy, Jay, and Rocko. It's like we don't exist. Do you know Jay had the nerve to say he's taking my baby? And that him and Endy are going to raise the kids together?" YaYa said as her eyes filled with tears.

"What?! Are you serious, girl? Roc told my mother the same thing, but she said she's going to fight him with everything in her to keep my babies in New York," Taiya said hopefully.

"Well, I heard through the grapevine that they are in town," YaYa told her.

"What? How'd you hear that?"

"Lynasia!"

"Oh, really? Well, KiKi has been acting really funny lately," Taiya responded. "She doesn't come visit no more or answer my calls."

"Maybe because she be around Marilyn so much. They don't approve of her talking to us. How about Evelyn told Jay that she will see Lil' Jay when he gets home? She didn't say anything like that for Endy's baby. I bet she's on her way to go see Endy's baby right now."

"Girl, don't worry about that. They'll get what's coming to them. You just make sure you don't let Jay think he's going to push your baby to the side like he doesn't exist," Taiya said.

"Oh, you know I'm not. I just hate that we can't be civil parents. What people fail to realize is that I didn't get pregnant alone," YaYa spat.

"Martin! Time's up!" a female guard yelled.

"Well, I gotta go. Keep me posted on everything, and you keep your head up out there," said Taiya as she stood to return to her cell.

"I will, babe. You do the same. Be back real soon."

YaYa hugged her and left.

AFTER THE BETRAYAL

As soon as she got into her car, YaYa looked at her phone and saw she had several missed calls from Keosha. Speaking of the devil. Now, she wants to call me after I've been trying to get her all day. YaYa dialed her number to see what was so urgent.

"Hi, girl! We need to meet. Where you at?" Keosha yelled into the phone.

"I called your ass earlier for Taiya's visit. I'm leaving Queensboro Correction. What's going on? Is everything okay?"

"Yes. Meet me at Ki Sushi," Keosha said and hung up.

When YaYa got to the restaurant, she tried to call Keosha, but there was no answer. So, she went straight inside. While searching for her in the crowded restaurant, she heard someone call her name.

"YaYa!"

To her surprise, she turned to find Evelyn, Jasean's mother, seated at the table bordering the kitchen doorway. YaYa felt her insides warp. Why would Keosha set me up like this? she thought to herself while slowly walking over to the table.

"Hello, sweetheart. I wanted to sit down and talk to you, so I asked Keosha to help make it happen. I figured you wouldn't meet with me alone."

"Well, she could have told me. I would've met with you without the setup," YaYa replied in an aggressive tone.

"Oh, you feel set up? Wow! Well, I'm pretty sure Endy felt the same way in Miami."

"Ms. Ev, I don't know what this is about, but if you're not here to talk about Lil' Jay, then we have nothing else to discuss!"

YaYa jumped up from her seat.

"Hoe, sit your ass down. Now! I'm not one of these little girls out here. So, if you want

24

me to make a scene, bring it on. This is not what your little off-brand ass wants," Evelyn growled as she gritted her teeth.

YaYa looked around as she sat back down, realizing Evelyn was not joking with her.

Once YaYa was seated again, Evelyn handed her a Carter's bag and said, "First of all, here... Take this for my grandson."

"Thanks a lot, but what's this sit-down about?"

"You knew my son was married. Yet, you failed to protect yourself, so you ended up getting pregnant. I don't know what you thought was gonna come of this situation... But, honey, he's not leaving Endyia. He made a mistake being with you. He loves that girl and those kids more than anything. Now, I'm not saying he won't love Lil' Jay the same, but, honey, it's going to be a challenge. Why would you name that baby after him anyway? That's not going to make him want to be with you more than he wants to be with her."

"First, let me say that when a person does something more than once, it's far from being a mistake. He laid with me without protection, just like I did with him. So, why am I the only one getting blamed? All I asked was that my son—his only boy—be treated fairly."

"Oh, so you don't know, do you?" Evelyn giggled.

Yaya looked at her with a puzzled expression. "Know what? What are you talking about?"

"Honey, Endy had a nine-pound baby boy yesterday. So, see, he has two boys now who are almost two months apart. Making the boy a junior won't make Jasean love him any more than his other kids. Now, I'm going to say this one time—leave Endy and my grandchildren alone. You put yourself in this position, so deal with it. What you won't do is ruin the chances of me being a grandmother and having Endy move the kids to North Carolina. I'm going to need you to fall back, and in return, we will send you money weekly for the baby," Evenly ordered.

AFTER THE BETRAYAL

"Lady, are you crazy?!" YaYa screamed, jumping up from her seat again.

"Sit your ass down."

"No, I'm not sitting down. My child is not for sale. What kind of woman are you? Don't worry about my son; he doesn't need anything from y'all. You tell that bastard I'll see him in court. I can't believe this bullshit!"

YaYa stormed out of the restaurant as onlookers whispered to each other.

♦ ♥ ♦ RoyaltyCrowned ♦ ♥ ♦

Endy was in awe of her baby boy. Despite his resemblance to Jasean, she showered him with kisses. She knew all the family would be coming to see them in a few, so she called a nurse to come in and help her to the bathroom to freshen up. As she exited the bathroom, she felt a presence behind her. She turned around and was shocked at who was standing there.

"Hi, Endy."

"What's good, Ki Ki I mean Keosha?"

"I need to talk to you, Endy. It's some shit about to go down. I think we can work together and get the hell away from these Newmans for good," Keosha explained.

"How can I trust you? For all I know, Ev could have sent you up here on some BS," Endy replied curtly.

"I got some information you're gonna want to hear. I think we can help each other and rid ourselves of those cheating bastards," Keosha told her.

"I will hear you out, sweetheart, but don't get too excited, because I don't trust you," Endy said to her straight up.

"After all is said and done, you're going to be happy you did," Keosha responded as she sat down in the chair next to the hospital bed.

"Like I said, I will hear you out. Go ahead and speak your peace," Endy said, giving her a doubtful look.

NEVA END

Chapter 4

What should have been a joyous time for Endy was becoming unsettling. For the last couple of days, Endy had been overprotective of her baby boy because she had been getting prank calls at the hospital. "Keep that little bastard close to you." "You better watch your baby." Those are the things the caller would say. She didn't even trust the nurses when they wanted to take her baby to the nursery so she could get some rest. Endy filed a report with the police, but there was no way they could prove Jasean or YaYa were the ones harassing her. The calls came from a library in Queens. The threats made her paranoid, so she requested a family member be with her around the clock. Keosha had informed her that Jasean tried to plan an ambush at the hospital with CPS. Jasean could be a devious bastard when he wanted to be, so she had to be cautious.

Niema and Rocko made it just in time to hear Endy curse out the prank caller when they arrived in New York. They decided to get a hotel nearby and stay by her side 24/7. Niema even told Endy that YaYa called her and knew she had the baby. So, her gut feeling told her that it was YaYa calling the hospital.

"I want out of this place! They said if I'm okay, I can go home today. I don't trust too many people right now," Endy stated.

"Don't rush it, though. We need to make sure you and the baby are okay. Remember, we got your back. We will be here every day until you go home...if need be," Niema told her.

"I'm ready to get to the crib," Endy groaned.

"I see we're all packed and ready to go," Tanya said as she entered the hospital room along with Evelyn.

"Yes, y'all. I'm ready for some food, family time, and a damn glass of wine," Endy replied, laughing.

"It's good to see that smile again!" Tanya joyfully remarked as she kissed Endy's cheek.

"Jay said to tell you all that he loves y'all and will see everyone soon," Evelyn said as she glanced at Endy. "He also said that you didn't want him to tell me the baby's name—that you wanted to do it. So, what is it?"

"Peace. His name is Peace."

"Peace?" Tanya asked, confused.

"Peace, like peace on Earth?" Evelyn asked.

"Yes, y'all! Peace. P–E–A–C–E," Endy replied.

"Well, we got Patience, and now we got Peace. God be with my babies. Y'all young parents don't know what to name these babies," Tanya commented, shaking her head and laughing.

"Our poor babies are going to be teased in school," Evelyn added, joining her in laughing.

AFTER THE BETRAYAL

Five days later, after Endy's blood pressure dropped to normality, the doctors came in with the discharge paperwork, finally giving Endy the green light to leave the hospital. The family had planned a small baby shower, and they were looking forward to the opportunity to surprise her.

After gathering Endy and the baby's things, they headed out of the hospital room. Yet, as they were leaving, they were the ones greeted with a surprise.

"What's good, Auntie?"

Endy looked up to see Jasean's cousin Caine, who was also Niema's ex.

"Hi, CJ. What are you doing here?" Evelyn asked. "I thought I told you Endy was going home today."

"I wanted to bring something for Lil' Junior since I won't be at the baby shower," Caine replied, handing Endy a gift bag.

"Thanks, CJ. That's so nice of you. Glad you're home with your baby," said Endy.

"Endy, I know I'm the last person you want to see, but I did want to say congratulations. I hope you can forgive me in the future... especially with all of us being family now," Caine replied.

"We have to see about that family stuff. Family doesn't condone fuck-boy behavior."

Tanya loudly cleared her throat and said, "Well, we got to go. My family is waiting for us to bring this precious boy home, so if you will excuse us."

"Yeah, Caine, tell your mother I will speak with her later. We do need to get to Lu's house before she starts calling," Evelyn added, shooting a mean look at Tanya.

"A'ight, y'all. Make moves then. Oh, Endy, if you and the kids ever need anything, just hit me up."

Caine hugged everyone but Tanya, who brushed past him.

30

"We'll be seeing you, Caine," Tanya called back as she pushed Endy along the hall.

As they faded out of sight, Caine stood there feeling conflicted about everything going on, especially since he and Endy used to be close. There was just so much drama.

"If she knew I saved her and her baby's life, she would be thanking me. Jay gotta get from behind them walls ASAP," he mumbled to himself.

◆ ❤ ◆ RoyaltyCrowned ◆ ❤ ◆

"I can't believe this bitch had the nerve to threaten me," YaYa ranted to Lynasia, pacing back and forth.

"Well, you know Endy and Ev are very close. Ev knows if Endy wanted to, she could take Jay for all he's got. I'm surprised she didn't, especially for him to have a whole damn baby."

"Alright...but the same thing happened with Ny and Roc. Ny had the nerve to judge me when she did the same shit to Taiya. Why is my situation looked at differently?"

"Girl, all I'm saying is you don't want no mess with them people. Between the Newmans, Perezes, and Hintons, they will always be one step ahead of you. With Ev and Marilyn, you have to be careful what you do to Jay and CJ. If you don't, you will learn the true meaning of a quiet storm," Lynasia warned her.

"I'm not scared of them old ladies. I'm suing Jay's tail for child support. I won't raise my baby by myself, Nay."

"Suit yourself. I'm saying... if they're offering to give you money, take it. Damn. You can't force Jay to be with you by holding child support over his head."

"Forget that! He's not gonna just get me pregnant and make my baby grow up with no father!"

YaYa's rage-filled screams turned into uneven sobs.

"Baby, he's married and wants to be with his wife. There's nothing you can do about that. What you can do is give that little boy all the love in the world."

Lynasia wrapped her arm around YaYa to comfort her.

"I just thought maybe after he saw his baby boy, he would have a change of heart and want to be a family."

"Let it go. You can't continue to do this to yourself. Pick yourself up and move on. Don't make trouble for yourself that you don't need. Move on, sis."

YaYa stopped crying and wiped her tears.

"Lynasia, I don't even know how."

◆ ♥ ◆ RoyaltyCrowned ◆ ♥ ◆

"Jasean Newman!" the guard yelled.

Jasean entered the visiting area and saw Caine waiting for him. They greeted each other with a hug and sat down.

"What up? Everything good?" Jasean asked anxiously.

"Yeah. Just wanted to check in on you. I saw your little man. He's your twin, yo!"

"Really? That's what's up! I told y'all I'm good. Y'all don't have to come see me so much."

"I know, man, but I'm not feeling you still being in here. Endy's moving real funny and has been MIA a lot. I wanted to tell you so you could be on guard."

"Endy ain't going nowhere. She's just upset. I know I got some making up to do. That's why my focus is on getting home."

"Well, this lawyer gotta make some moves. You don't want to come home to your child being around another man. She goes back and forth to Carolina a lot, I heard. How's everything going with YaYa? She not tripping, is she?" Caine asked.

"She tried to pull some shit about us being a family, but her ass knew what the situation was when she entered this. I'm not leaving my family for no chick out here. She's threatening to sue me for child support, but I told my mom to talk to her. Trying to see if we can settle this out of court."

"Yeah, KiKi told me. She on some other bullshit, so what you gon' do about it? Do you need me to handle it?"

"No, I'm good, cuz. I want to go for full custody because you know E isn't about to let me have no contact with that girl. I can't just leave my son, though, man."

"Yo, man, that's gon' be your best bet. She's talking really reckless. I feel like she will try some crazy shit with your seed—like going back to New Orleans. Just focus on getting out of here, and I'll keep my ears open. I got your back, cuz. You know that."

"That chick not stupid enough to take my son out of state," Jasean assured him.

"Alright, if you say so. Just know that I got your back with whatever you need. Just give me the green light, and I'm ready," Caine stated.

"Just look out for my family. I got the rest when I get out of here in a few days," Jasean gritted.

◆ ❤ ◆ RoyaltyCrowned ◆ ❤ ◆

When Endy arrived at her grandmother's house, she was excited to see all her family together again.

"Is that my nephew?!" Lisa hollered from the stoop.

Endy laughed. "Y'all crazy. Couldn't even wait for us to get in the house."

"Girl, you know we been ready. Nana wouldn't let us come to the hospital, saying you needed to rest. So, I got here first to be the first one to hold Peace!" Egypt said while giving her cousin a tight hug.

"I know. I'm just messing with y'all."

"Especially when we were thinking we would be welcoming a baby girl, and it was a boy all along," Chynna added, also hugging her.

AFTER THE BETRAYAL

"Girl, who you telling? I was in shock but happy as hell, too," Endy confessed.

"Y'all let her get in the house so she can get the baby out this air," Luella hollered as she brushed away the circle that formed around Endy and the baby.

When they entered the house, Endy was surprised at how fast her family threw together the beautiful baby shower. It was a Mickey Mouse theme with bright-colored balloons and decorations. They initially wanted to rent a party hall, but the uncertainty around YaYa's intentions made it a risky plan.

"So, Endy... have you talked to Jasean today?" Asia asked.

"You know he's calling back-to-back. I just want to spend time with y'all right now. He and I can talk later. All that mess is irrelevant at this point," Endy replied.

"I just want you to know we're all here and will chip in where we need to, cuz," Egypt told her.

"Aww, thanks so much, y'all. But believe me, I got everything situated. I'm gon' give myself a few weeks off, and then back to work I go."

"A few weeks? Girl, you're tripping. Did you see what happened to you after the baby? You have to take it easy. That blood pressure is nothing to mess with. E-Class is not going anywhere, and neither is the club. You have to take care of yourself first, sweetheart. Work is gon' be there," Chynna sternly lectured.

"Okay, mother," Endy replied, being sarcastic. "I know that, but I'm telling you that I'm as good as can be," she assured Chynna.

"That's right. I'm gon' be on your tail like white on rice until I think you're listening to me."

"Well, let's say grace so we can get to this food before it gets cold," Luella said and headed toward the dining room.

A knock at the door pulled everyone out of their reverie.

"I got it. Go 'head," Chynna told Endy.

"Chy, see who it is. It might be Keosha. I invited her," Endy said.

Chynna opened the door. "Marilyn! KiKi! What's going on?"

"It's all good, Chynna. Let them in. One thing I'm starting to realize is, regardless of how we feel about each other, we're going to have to be around each other at some point. So, why not get the shit over with?" Endy said and walked away.

Meanwhile, Chynna stood there with a confused expression on her face.

"Thanks," both women curtly said as they entered the house.

Although there had been tension with everyone over the last year or so, Endy felt it was time everyone made peace once and for all.

"Y'all, we have more guests joining us," Endy announced to the rest of the family.

When Chynna entered the dining room with Marilyn and Keosha, everyone looked like they had sucked a lemon. Niema shot Chynna and Endy a disapproving look.

Eventually, Luella broke the ice. "Well, thanks for coming to celebrate our newest addition, Peace Hinton Newman."

"You know I'm ready to see my nephew. I know he's a cutie. Well, hello, Ny. I didn't know you were still in town. I was hoping I'd see you," Marilyn said as she walked over to hug her.

Keosha grunted, clearly showing her discomfort.

"Roc, go ahead and say grace," Luella told him when she noticed his mood turn sour upon Marilyn and Keosha's arrival.

After dinner, the family was laughing and talking while oldies but goodies tunes played in the background. Niema was not happy about Keosha being around, but as Endy said, there was no need to try to dodge each other. Although she was very much in love with Rocko, she still couldn't wrap her head around the whole Caine and Keosha having a baby ordeal. She and Rocko also had a baby, but she still couldn't accept that Caine had a baby on her after all the years they shared. Then he ended up in a relationship with

AFTER THE BETRAYAL

Keosha. Never in a million years did she think her life would end up like this.

"Ma, you good?" Rocko asked as he walked up behind Niema and kissed her softly on the neck.

She loved when he did that because his cologne was so intoxicating to her. They were deeply in love with each other, and it showed. So much so that Marilyn even watched them in admiration, wishing her son Caine wasn't such an asshole.

"Endy, girl, the baby is gorgeous. You got to let me keep him sometimes," Egypt said, sniffing Peace's fresh baby smell.

"Believe me, you will be getting called a lot--you and Rizzy. You know Asia's tail has no damn patience," Endy laughed.

"Whatever, Endy. Y'all kids are my birth control. Ha, ha, ha," Asia shot back.

"Chynna, can you come here for a minute?" Asia said suddenly, alarming her.

"Everything okay, boo?" Endy asked.

"Yeah, I just need Chy to look at something for the dance studio," Asia replied.

Chynna followed her to the kitchen and then out the back door.

"What's up?"

"Girl, why did YaYa post the baby on Facebook?"

"So?" Chynna responded, confused.

"She tagged Jay in the damn pictures, saying Daddy's twin."

Asia held the phone up to show her.

"Oh, shit. Endy's gon' bug the hell out," Chynna panicked.

"What y'all back here talking about?" Ari asked as she strolled up to them.

"Bitch, I'm gon' hurt you," Asia laughed.

"What's going on, y'all? Spill the beans," Ari insisted, knowing they were trying to hide something from her.

"Okay, we will tell you, but promise us that you will not get all crazy and shit because we don't need Endy upset," Chynna warned.

"Okay, girl. What is it?"

"Bam!" Asia said as she pushed the phone up to her face.

"Umm, I know this thot did not post this on Facebook?" Ari asked, hoping she was dreaming.

"We need to talk to Ev so she can get Jay's side hoe in check," Chynna huffed.

"Well, that is her baby's father, too," Asia groaned.

"Girl, fuck her. It's not the time to try to be relevant," Ari snapped.

"How will we get Ev out here without Endy getting suspicious?" Chynna asked.

The girls decided to text Ev to come around back, which is exactly what Ev did.

"Ladies, I already know what's going on. All my family in Miami is calling and texting Marilyn and me. I don't want Endy stressed, so please make sure she's good while I go handle this," Evelyn said, dialing her phone.

"Yo, chicken heads, everything good? Endy is looking for y'all," Niema said, joining them.

"Yeah, everything is fine. I'm about to head out to make some runs, but I will be back this evening before it gets too late," Evelyn stated, then hugged everyone. She had prepared to leave to go and check YaYa on her bullshit.

"Y'all sure everything is okay, guys?" Niema asked again.

"Yeah, girl... everything is good. We were just saying how we all need to be here for Endy more than ever right now," Chynna quickly responded as Ev made a beeline for the front door.

"I wish I could stay longer, but I need to get back to look at some office spaces," Niema explained.

"We know y'all have a new life in North Cakalack. Y'all done went south on us," Karishma joked.

AFTER THE BETRAYAL

"Yup! I'm enjoying it, too. We have lots of shopping centers near us and a good amount of land for the kids to run and play."

Everyone talked and laughed as Endy pulled out her phone to record the shower on Facebook. She stopped short when she noticed a heart-wrenching image appear on her feed. Her face contorted into agony, and her heartbeat raced uncontrollably as she read the caption: Daddy's twin. That sent Endy in a rage; she was ready to kick YaYa's ass at that point.

"So, why the hell didn't anybody tell me this hoe tagged Jay in a picture of her baby?" Endy shouted, startling everyone.

"Endy, we didn't want you getting upset with your high blood pressure and all," Ari explained calmly.

"Endy, I didn't know. I swear," Niema replied.

"This shit will never end. So, you know what? I'm going to play right along with this hoe. She's about to know who the hell I am!" Endy yelled, then stormed back into the house.

"This shit about to get really bad...really quick," Ari said as she shook her head.

FOR THE LOVE OF MONEY

Chapter 5

A few weeks had passed since the whole situation with YaYa, but Endy's anger still hadn't subsided. She woke up just as mad as the first day of the incident. Her family checked in on her daily, but she asked them for some space for a few days. She needed to be left alone for a while to figure out what she needed to do about her marriage. Part of her wanted to say forget everything and leave him. Another more sentimental part of her didn't want to leave all she had built with her husband and raise two kids alone. Endy had to figure out what she wanted to do—and sooner than later.

Endy picked up her vibrating cell phone, cleared her throat with a grunt, and gently said, "Hello," into the speaker. She was still a little groggy from her deep sleep.

"What's up, cuz? You still sleep?" Karishma asked.

"Nah, you good, Rizzy. I was just about to get myself together. I need to get up to go get the kids from Mommy house anyway," Endy said, jumping out of bed.

"Well, what time is the meeting?" Karishma asked.

"Oh, shoot! That is today! Damn it!" Endy shouted into the phone.

AFTER THE BETRAYAL

"Calm down, cuz. I got you. I'm on my way. We can put together a quick little brunch, and I'll pick it up. We have a couple of hours. You just get yourself together," Karishma told her.

"Okay. This meeting has to go right. My whole future is riding on this," Endy said nervously.

"Well, you get the house together. I'll tell Egypt to get the kids for a couple of hours until we finish. Everything will turn out fine, cuz."

Endy got quiet, feeling foolish. All her family did was try to help. She decided to chill out and accept her baby cousin's help.

"Okay, Rizzy, I'm going to let you handle it. I will see you when you get here," Endy said and hung up the phone.

Endy quickly jumped in the shower, threw on a pantsuit, and pulled her hair back in a sleek ponytail for the upcoming meeting.

◆ ♥ ◆ RoyaltyCrowned ◆ ♥ ◆

Ding, dong!

Endy gave herself a once-over before going to answer it. She opened the door to find Niema's Aunt Sally standing there.

"Hi, baby. I didn't mean to pop up on you, but I can never seem to catch you," Aunt Sally mumbled.

"Is everything alright?" Endy asked after she greeted her.

"I wanted to speak to you for a few minutes... if I can," she said.

"Auntie, I'm about to have a business meeting. Maybe I can come by and see you another time. I'm already running behind," Endy explained.

"Okay, I understand that, but I just want to say I apologize again for all the hurt my niece has caused. I know you're nowhere near forgiving her, but I pray God heals your heart. What YaYa has done is unexplainable, and I'm deeply sorry."

Aunt Sally looked like she was putting in effort to keep herself from crying, but eventually, the tears gave way on their own.

"It's okay. Everything is going to work itself out. God has me and my babies, so I have to believe everything will be okay. He will deal with Jay and YaYa in time. All I can do for all of us right now is pray, Auntie," Endy replied calmly.

"Hello, is this Endyia Newman's residence?" a woman asked from behind Aunt Sally, interrupting their conversation.

"Ms. Nina Shapiro, how are you doing? My aunt was just leaving," Endy said, smiling at Aunt Sally.

"Oh, yes...I was on my way out. I will talk to you later, Endy," Aunt Sally said and hugged Endy.

"Yes, I will be talking to you, Auntie. And, Ms. Shapiro, please come in," Endy told her as the woman stepped inside. "You can have a seat wherever you like," she said, signaling at the sitting room.

"Well, Ms. Newman, it's nice to finally meet you," Nina said as she made herself comfortable on the sofa. "And please, call me Nina. Now, how sure are you about this? Are you ready to get to work?"

"Nina, I've never been more ready to do anything in my life. Oh, and you can call me Endy. I have to protect myself and my children by any means necessary. It's now or never," Endy said, making it clear to her that she was fully prepared.

"Okay, let's do this. But once it's done, there is no turning back. You have to be all in," Nina explained.

"I'm all in. Will this be enough to get us started?"

AFTER THE BETRAYAL

Endy pulled out twenty-thousand dollars from a tote bag and placed it on the coffee table.

Nina couldn't believe her eyes. At that point, she knew Endy wasn't playing. She extended her hand to Endy to close the deal.

"Let's get it!" Endy cheered.

◆ ♥ ◆RoyaltyCrowned ◆ ♥ ◆

"Rizzy, is that you?" Caine called out.

"What's up, CJ?"

Noticing the food and baby products in Rizzy's hands, Caine asked, "Where you headed to?"

"A homegirl's house," Karishma answered casually.

"How's Endy doing? Jay said he hadn't spoken to her in a couple weeks. I hope she ain't tripping over that nonsense with YaYa."

"Tell your cousin that my cousins are doing just fine. I guess he will just have to talk to her when he gets home," she responded angrily.

"Okay, Rizzy, I hear you. Just know he will be home sooner than later," Caine said with a sly grin.

"Yeah, whatever!"

She quickly brushed past him and got into her car, after which she quickly dialed Chynna's number.

"Chy, this is Rizzy. Why did I just run into that shyster-ass jerk CJ downtown? He's talking like Jay will be home soon--"

"Rizzy, don't panic. Just get over to Endy's. I will meet you there in about an hour. She needs to let us help her through this mess, and I'm not taking no for an answer," Chynna said, fed up.

"Okay, I'll see you when you get there. Love you," Karishma said before hanging up.

She cranked up her car and proceeded to Endy's house. After calming herself down, she got the food out of the car and rang the doorbell.

"Come on in, Rizzy!" Endy yelled out.

Noticing Karishma struggling to find her balance as she carried the bags, Endy got up to help her.

"Wow! You are gorgeous! And those eyes!" Nina gushed over Karishma.

"Aww, thanks. You're beautiful yourself!" Karishma said shyly.

"Okay, okay...we're all gorgeous. Can we get some food popping?" Endy whined.

"Yeah, greedy," Karishma laughed.

They started to dig into the exclusive brunch Endy had catered for them. There were waffles, omelets—filled with turkey bacon, cheese, onions, and peppers—hash browns, grits, and toast.

Ding, dong!

"Got it!" Karishma yelled as she jumped up to answer the door.

"What the hell do you want?" Karishma spazzed when she spotted Keosha standing at the doorway.

"Can I please talk to Endy? It's something she needs to know. This is very important."

"Who is it, Rizzy?" Endy walked up behind her, becoming startled at the person in view. "Keosha? What are you doing here? How do you know where I live? Never mind. Of course, CJ told you. What am I thinking? I know I said I would let bygones be bygones, but this is extreme... showing up at my crib like this."

"I know I shouldn't have popped up, but I need to tell you something. It's about Jay. It concerns the kids, and I think you should know," Keosha blurted out.

"What about my kids?"

"Can I come in and talk to you? I know if it was me, I would want someone to let me know. I just need a few minutes."

"Come in. This better not be no bullshit, Keosha."

"It's not. I promise you will thank me later," she assured Endy.

"Well, we should pick this up later," Nina jumped up.

"No, you're fine. I'm sure this will only take a minute," Endy told her.

"Okay, first off, Jay will be home Monday with an ankle monitor and curfew. They're still trying to gather evidence for the charges. The case has gotten deep, and Jay is trying to go out with a bang. He's talking about taking the kids and businesses from you if you don't take him back. They are plotting against you. Me, as a mother, I can't let him and CJ sabotage you like this. He's the one who fucked up."

"Wait, so if I don't take him back, he's going to try to take the businesses and the kids? Really? Like I'm the one who screwed up the marriage? Are you freaking kidding me? This bastard is bugging! Dead ass!" Endy screamed.

"Sorry, I was so mean earlier, KiKi... I mean, Keosha. Thanks for letting us know that. You know them Newmans have a mean streak, especially when it comes to their family," Karishma said.

"Well, we are Hintons, and we don't play about our family either! So, Jasean and his cousin can kiss my ass. They want to go to war, then to war we will go! I'll be damned if they take my babies."

"Endy, this is your confirmation, honey. You can get everything if you just chill and let me and my team handle it," Nina advised.

"Okay, I'm going to let you handle it, but just know that I'm going after everything now. You want to play with me, Mr. Newman? Let the games begin."

◆ ❤ ◆ RoyaltyCrowned ◆ ❤ ◆

"You have a call from—"

"Jasean!"

"An inmate at Clinton Correction Facility."

"This is Jay right here. I'm letting him know what his wife is out here doing—not answering my calls, texts, or inboxes. You know she blocked me and Jay from Facebook and Instagram?" Evelyn said to Marilyn.

"Hey, Ma, what's good?" Jasean said.

"Baby, Endy is not budging! That shit YaYa pulled pissed her off. I understand her being upset, but she can't take this out on me. I want to see my grandkids, and she won't even let Tanya or the family step foot there. I need to know what's going on with those kids," Evelyn cried.

"Ma, chill. I'll be home in a few days. I'ma handle it," Jasean assured her.

"In the meantime, I've been seeing Lil' Jay. That boy looks just like you. I haven't seen Peace or Patience in almost three weeks, though!"

"I know, Ma. Endy is upset right now, so she's gon' do anything to hurt me. She knows I want you to see the kids as much as possible. So, this is her way of getting back at me, that's all."

"I don't care what you and her have going on! That has nothing to do with us seeing the kids, Jay," Evelyn cried out.

"Ma, please, just let me handle it. Don't do no stupid shit to make things worse. I want my family back. I don't need nonsense going on while I'm in here."

"Patience's birthday is on Monday. How are we gon' celebrate it if Endy won't even talk to us?" Evelyn asked.

"I will be home by then, Ma. We will celebrate with her. Just sit back and chill. Trust me, once I get home, everything will be okay," he said, trying hard to maintain an optimistic tone.

AFTER THE BETRAYAL

"Okay, son, I will let you handle your family affairs. But if I don't see my grandbaby for her birthday, I got something for both of y'all," Evelyn snarled, handing Marilyn the phone.

"Hi, baby."

"Hi, Auntie. How you doing?"

"I'm good. Trying to keep your mother under control. You know she's about ready to pull up on Endy," Marilyn responded, laughing.

"I know she is, but we have to handle this another way. I don't want to make no mistakes that will make me not be able to see my kids at all. Please keep my mom calm," Jasean begged.

"I got you, baby. Just keep your head up. See you when you get home. We gon' celebrate," Marilyn said, trying to lift his spirits.

"Yes, we are. But until then, y'all hold it down. Tell CJ that I'm gon' hit him up later."

Jasean said his goodbyes and hung up.

"God, please get me to my family. Please, get me out of here before it's too late," Jasean prayed.

"Ev, why did you do that to that boy?" Marilyn screamed at her.

"I want to see my grandchildren! Is that so wrong?"

"No, it's not, but that girl is hurting. Her husband had a baby by someone she thought was a friend to him or at least cool enough with her not to cross that line. Then she named the baby after Jay, and to top it off, he's locked up, leaving her to pick up the pieces alone. That's a lot, Ev, and you know it," Marilyn spoke seriously and truthfully.

"Aye, you worry about CJ and Keosha, and let me worry about my son and grandkids."

"Okay, but you know if you try some bullshit, it's only going to make Jay upset with you. All I'm saying is let that boy live his life."

"I'm calling Tanya. If anybody can talk to Endy, it's her," Evelyn said, searching around for her phone.

"I know you're not gonna call that woman!" Marilyn said sarcastically.

"Yes. Yes, I am. Who gonna stop me? Somebody needs to talk some sense into Endy before this situation gets crazy. I won't go without seeing my grandchildren because of her and Jay's mess. I miss seeing those babies," Evelyn cried.

"Ev, let them handle it. Please just stay out of it," Marilyn begged her sister.

"I will for now, but if we don't get invited to Patience's birthday party, all hell is gon' break loose. I'm not playing," stated Evelyn as she stormed out the living room.

AFTER THE BETRAYAL

A PARTY AIN'T A PARTY

Chapter 6

"**C**hile, please tell me you did not post that baby on the internet to taunt that girl!" Aunt Sally shouted.

"Yeah. What about it? Why is it such a big deal if I want to post my son? He's Jay's son, and he won't be treated like an outcast. I'm not ashamed of shit!" YaYa barked back.

"YaYa, are you freaking serious right now?! You have created beef with three families because of your selfish intentions. As usual, you're doing what the hell you want to do. Try having some self-respect for once! Like, damn, you messed around and had a baby by a married man who happens to be my best friend's husband. Don't you think you've done enough damage?" Niema yelled, ready to pounce on YaYa.

"Oh, so you're going to fight me--your own flesh and blood--over people who don't give a damn about you?! You have spent most of your life chasing them people. You're not perfect, Ny! You have your shit, too! Rocko was in a relationship with someone, as well!"

"Yeah, bitch... a relationship, not a marriage!" Niema shouted and shoved YaYa.

"Y'all stop this mess now! We are family whether you like it or not, and we're gon'

48

start acting like it!" Aunt Sally yelled.

"Aunt Sally, I'm gon' go 'head and leave before I slap your niece. She's not my family either. Family don't cross you like she's done me."

Niema coldly fixated her gaze at YaYa before turning her back to walk out.

"Ny, please don't leave! We have to resolve this before it's too late. Please don't leave like this!" Aunt Sally begged.

"Aunt Sally, I have to go before this gets out of hand. I'm done trying to reason with her. She's selfish and self-centered. She doesn't understand the severity of what she has done!" Niema screamed.

"Go run to your made-up family!" YaYa teased maliciously.

"Auntie, I'ma go on and leave before I whip her ass in here. I only came because you asked me to. I will be back before I go back down South."

"Niyana, I don't know what you're thinking, but you better humble yourself, sweetie. God don't like what you're doing. You made this mess, so you better find a way to fix it—and quick!" Aunt Sally snarled at her.

"Seriously?! Y'all want me to hide my son while those other two babies get to be paraded around and showered with love?! Hell no! Jay is going to treat and love Jasean Jr. just like he does Patience and his other child."

"You can't make that man accept a baby. YaYa, you brought this all on yourself. You're playing with fire, little girl, and your baby is the only person who is going to get burned."

◆ ♥ ◆ RoyaltyCrowned ◆ ♥ ◆

Even though Jasean wasn't there to help plan the party, it didn't stop Endy from going all out for her baby girl's first birthday party. Luella kept the kids while Endy, her mother, and her cousins went shopping for everything to give Patience a Disney-themed birthday party.

AFTER THE BETRAYAL

"I just received a text from Evelyn asking what the plans are for Patience's birthday," Tanya told Endy as she stared at her phone's screen.

"Mommy, ignore it. I don't feel like dealing with them today. Jay is out on bail, and I know he's gonna come with them. I want to enjoy my baby's birthday with family and friends. No drama," she replied.

"I think that's a little extreme not to let them come for the baby's first birthday party, Endy. That is her father and grandmother. Do it for Patience; forget the rest. You can't blame them for what YaYa did on social media," Chynna advised her.

"I said what I said," Endy stated firmly.

When Endy refocused her attention on the shopping, Lisa approached her sister and whispered, "Tanya, just let her be. I don't blame her for not wanting that negative energy at her baby's party. When she's ready to deal with it, she will. Just don't push her."

"Okay, I'm going to let her handle it, but you know Ev is not going to give up. Especially with this being her first grandbaby's birthday party. You know how much she loves that girl."

"Well, I feel like we should let her handle it," Lisa said sternly, fed up with Tanya's obsession with controlling Endy.

Ring! Ring! Ring!

"Hello?"

"Chynna, what up? Where Endy at? This Jay."

"Hmm."

Chynna stood stunned with the phone held against her ear.

"Who is it, Chynna?" Tanya asked.

"It's Jay. He wants Endy."

"Damn, all this bullshit! Gimme the damn phone," Tanya yelled as she grabbed the device out of Chynna's loose grip and handed it to Endy.

"Ma, really?" Endy growled.

"Talk to your husband. This is not our fight."

Endy shot Tanya a mean look, hung up the phone, and said, "Ma, why would you do that? I told you I don't want to talk to him right now."

"Endy! Come on now! That was uncalled for! I know you're upset, but don't make him miss his baby's first birthday," Chynna argued.

"You know what? Just invite them all. Invite Jay, Ev, Marilyn, Caine, Keosha, Cadence, and while you're at it, invite YaYa and Lil' Jasean! Let's just make it one big family affair. I'm going to be the bigger person and let them come to the party. It's about Patience, not me. Text them the address, but one sign of bullshit, and they are getting put out."

The crew stood in silence, then busted out laughing.

"Y'all, if that ain't a replica of Tanya Hinton right there..." Lisa remarked sarcastically.

"Bougie hood," Egypt added.

"Why yo' ass ain't put her in her place?" Lisa asked Tanya.

"I ain't messing with Endy right now. If I did, I would've been done smacked her in her damn mouth. They done unleashed the beast. I'm staying out the way," Tanya said as she threw her hands up in the air.

"Y'all better leave my niece alone. She not playing with y'all," Lisa chuckled.

"Fuck you! Endy will get her butt whipped messing with me."

In a singsong voice, Lisa began to repeat, "I told you so."

◆ ♥ ◆ RoyaltyCrowned ◆ ♥ ◆

"Aye, Ma! Where you been?" Rocko asked Niema as she plopped down on the sofa in their hotel room.

"I just left my aunt's house from a so-called intervention with YaYa. I still didn't get to see the baby," Niema replied while leaning over to kiss him.

AFTER THE BETRAYAL

"Word? Last year was one hell of a year. Shit crazy for real, yo. Just give it some time, babe," Rocko said as he wrapped his arms around her.

"I know. I just hate that it had to be my cousin who started all this mess. Like how low can you get? Babe, get this. She's not even remorseful about it. It's like she's getting a kick out of this whole shit," Niema's voice crackled as her emotions overcame her.

"Ny, come on... no crying today. We gonna enjoy our trip here. Let it go. In due time, all this shit will work out somehow. Trust me," Rocko said while rubbing her back.

"You don't get it, babe. When Endy hurts, I hurt. She doesn't deserve this. YaYa betrayed me in the foulest way possible."

"I know, babe. We just gotta pray for everyone involved. That's all we can do at this point," Rocko told her, then gently kissed her lips.

"I love you so much, babe," Niema said as she cradled his face, kissing him back.

"You better stop before I put another one in you," exclaimed Rocko, jumping up off the sofa.

"Do it then, Papi," Niema teased as she stretched out her body for Rocko to gaze at lustfully.

Rocko looked her up and down a few times before reaching out his hands to pull her up to him.

"Later. We need to leave now before we be late for this party."

Knock, knock!

"Who knows we're here?" Niema asked.

"All my family! Can you get it while I finish getting dressed?" Rocko told her as he made his way to the bedroom.

Knock, knock, knock, knock!

"Sure, babe"

Bam, bam, bam!

"Okay! I'm coming! Who is beating at the door like that? Geez Louise," Niema yelled as she snatched open the door.

"It's me! We need to get to Nana's house! Ev and them are on the way there. Keosha just called me!" Karishma shouted frantically as she rushed into their hotel room.

"Keosha? When did y'all become so friendly?" Niema questioned with a frown.

"Since she been filling Endy in on what's going on with Jay and his treacherous family."

"What you mean they on the way to Ma's house? I know they don't want no shit today. Let's go now," Rocko told them both.

They raced to their vehicles and headed straight to Brooklyn. When they arrived, they saw Evelyn's car parked out front of Luella's house.

"These motherfuckers better leave Ma out this nonsense," Rocko barked as he jumped out of the car.

"Roc, just chill. Don't go in there flexing. Let's see what's going on first, please," Niema pleaded.

Her words went in one ear and out the other. Before they knew it, he was already racing up the steps to the front door of Luella's brownstone. Rocko rushed through the door, expecting to find his mother in a tense argument with Ev. To his surprise, he found Luella, Marilyn, and Evelyn sitting in the living room idly talking.

"Boy, what's your problem? Why you rushing in my house like that?" Luella asked, unamused.

"I was making sure you were good, Ma," Rocko said, his eyes darting between Evelyn and Marilyn.

"Yeah, I'm good. What's wrong with you?"

"I know Endy said she didn't invite Jay to the party. So, I wanted to see why Evelyn was here and what her agenda was coming to see you," he replied, unconsciously nudging his chin towards Evelyn and Marilyn.

"Boy, I called them over here so we can reach some type of peace with this situation. Evelyn is still those kids' grandmother, and she shouldn't be punished for Jay's actions," Luella explained.

Rocko knew she was right, but he didn't want Endy to feel betrayed.

"Ma, let me holla at you in the kitchen."

Rocko walked off; Luella stood up and followed behind him.

"Ma, what are you doing? Endy is going to flip out if they show up to the party! I think y'all need to let her handle this on her own," Rocko whispered angrily as soon as Luella entered the kitchen.

"Look, I understand you want to support your cousin. But wrong is wrong, and right is right. Endy is wrong for not allowing Evelyn to see her grandbabies. She can't take what he did out on everyone. She needs to suck that shit up and hold her head high. Karma will deal with Jay and YaYa. With that being said, I know what I'm doing. I got this."

Luella patted his right cheek and headed back into the living room, but before she could take her spot on the sofa, Tanya was walking into the room.

"Hello, ladies! I'm so glad y'all are here. As you know, Endy did not invite y'all to the party at first, but she's had a change of heart and wants y'all to come," announced Tanya with a smile.

"Hallelujah!" Luella cried out.

"I'm so glad she changed her mind! I didn't want to miss my first grandbaby's birthday. I love Endy," Evelyn expressed. "You know that, Tanya. I wish I could take her pain away... I do. But this is beyond my control."

"I know this has been an emotional rollercoaster. Please know we understand and just want to celebrate Patience," Marilyn added.

Karishma, Rocko, and Niema walked in right in the middle of everything.

"I'm sorry, Ny. I'm sorry the men we birthed have caused y'all so much pain, but please know I love you and Endy," Marilyn cried.

Niema began to get teary-eyed, but Rocko wasn't fazed one bit by their tears.

"Okay, I'm going to head over to Highland Park. We'll let Endy know that y'all are not to be blamed for Jay's actions and that y'all have both Endy and the babies' best interest at heart. Oh, and to let her know Jay might show up," Tanya explained to Marilyn and Evelyn.

"I see this is about to be a crazy day," sighed Rocko.

◆ ♥ ◆ RoyaltyCrowned ◆ ♥ ◆

Patience's birthday party turned out to be just how Endy wanted it to be. Everyone enjoyed themselves, and the food was great. The kids had everything to do from face painting, a bounce house with waterslide, pony rides, magic show, carousel ride, cotton candy stand, Italian ice cart, grilled food, and much more. She even had security around for safekeeping. Endy knew she went a little overboard, but she didn't want any drama to overshadow her baby girl's first birthday.

"Girl, this party is nice as hell! You did that, best friend," Ari said as she ran up and hugged Endy.

Trailing behind Ari were her twin babies.

"Hi, Aunt Endy!" they chirped.

"Hi, my babies! I missed y'all. TJ looks just like his father, and Asia looks just like you. How is that possible?" Endy laughed as she kissed the twins.

"Ty, please make sure you keep your eyes on them!" Ari yelled.

"Ariana, I got them. Damn! They my kids, too. What up, Endy?" Tylon spoke.

"What's good, Ty? Don't let this chick agitate you. We know you got your babies," laughed Endy, then teasingly said, "Girl, hmm, what is Tylon doing? Because my brother is looking fit and young these days."

AFTER THE BETRAYAL

"Bitch, too damn young! I'm worried, sis. He's been on this health and fitness kick. When I argue with him, he doesn't even argue back; he just leaves. He's been planning playdates with the twins and not including me. I'm telling you, he's been really distant lately," Ari explained.

"Well, Ari, maybe y'all need to talk to someone. Have you tried communicating with him about how you feel? You have a good husband, girl. You better see what's on his mind."

"I know, Endy. It's been nagging the hell out of me. I knew you were going through your own bullshit, so I didn't want to bring it to you. You know you're our Iyanla Vanzant," Ari laughed.

"Girl, forget you. I've been on some positive vibes and energy-type shit. I'm not tolerating no nonsense from no man ever again."

"Sis, don't let that situation tear you down. You are a strong, Black woman who's got a lot to offer. Baby, you're blessed. Now, if you want your marriage, you know you got that in the bag, but if you want to let it go, then let it go. Whatever you decide to do, I'm with you either way," Ari whispered, hugging her again.

"I know, sis. Well, it's no time for tears. I have to enjoy this day for my princess."

Endy knew she had to keep it together for her baby girl. So, she sucked it up and headed over to see Patience, who was sitting on the pony smiling from ear to ear. Everyone took pictures and had a great time, especially the children.

"Endy, I want you to chill and don't show out," Chynna said as she ran up to her.

Before Endy could react, she looked up and saw Luella walking in with Evelyn, Marilyn, and Jasean in tow. She was in shock because she couldn't believe Jasean had been released in time.

"Now, cuz, you got to keep it together for the kids' sake," Chynna told her when she saw Endy's angered look with Jasean's presence. "You can't turn that man away from his baby's first birthday party. Plus, he hasn't seen his son yet. You got to respect him for even coming after what he's done--"

"Whatever! I don't feel no sympathy for his cheating, sorry ass. I'm not dealing with him at all," Endy barked.

"Endyia. Hi, baby girl. Everything looks really nice," Luella said, trying to act normal.

"Hi, Nana. Thanks for coming. I was about to go check on the birthday cake," Endy responded, wanting to rush off.

"Endy, please don't be rude. They are still the children's family," Luella begged. "They need to be here. Don't let your stubbornness ruin Patience's Day."

Meanwhile, Jasean raced over to Tanya, who was holding Peace in her arms. He hadn't seen his son since he was born and couldn't wait to hold him.

"Endy, baby, please know that I'm on your side when it comes to this situation. I just wanted to celebrate my grandchild's first birthday with her. I'm not here to cause trouble or argue with you. I love you. Please understand that," Evelyn explained.

"I don't have no beef with you, Ma Ev. I just really can't deal with Jay today. I wanted a peaceful day with my babies. That's it."

"I promise we just want to sing happy birthday and leave," Marilyn jumped in.

"Hell, he might as well stay. It didn't really matter how I felt! What I say don't mean shit!" Endy yelled and stormed off.

Jasean raced behind her.

"E, yo! Hold up."

"What is it, Jay? Spend time with your kids and leave me the hell alone!"

"Endy, I'm sorry. I don't know what I need to do to show you how sorry I am."

"Dude, this is not the time nor the place to be talking about this shit. Just leave me alone!"

"Jay, just let her be and spend time with your daughter and son. This is your baby's birthday, so let her enjoy it. I will talk to her," Tanya whispered to him.

AFTER THE BETRAYAL

"I'm sorry, Ma... E, you know I love you. I messed up big time. I know I did, but please find it in your heart to forgive me," he said, then walked off.

"Aye, y'all! We're ready to sing happy birthday! Are you good? Or do you need a few? I can tell them to give us a few more minutes," Asia said.

"Nah, I'm good, cuz. Let's get this over with. I have a lot of colleagues and customers here, and I don't want them to see me in a down mood," Endy sighed.

"Okay, you're ready. Let's go." Tanya encouraged.

When they got to the table, Jasean was already holding Patience and Peace with a big-ass smile on his face. Endy shot daggers at him with her eyes. She slowly walked over to them and put her game face on for the crowd.

"Okay, y'all, let's do this," she said and grabbed Patience out of his arms.

After they sang happy birthday, the photographers took pictures. Just like that, Endy felt like her family was complete. She was even feeling this crazy attraction to Jasean all of a sudden. He was smelling like Tom Ford, looking good as hell with a navy-blue Polo, dark blue denim True Religion jeans, and blue and white Air Force Ones. There was no doubt that she wanted to jump on him, but she knew it would be a bad idea. She enjoyed her family moment and let the thought go.

FALLIN'

Chapter 7

"**D**id you know this asshole is in New York? He didn't even go by to see the baby," Taiya yelled, attracting the attention of the guards.

"Aye, quiet down!" a guard shouted.

"Sorry about that, Reese," Taiya responded, fearing her visit would be cut short.

"Girl, chill out! I didn't come all the way here to get kicked out," Lynasia groaned.

"Me either," YaYa added.

"I know, y'all. Dang! Anyway, so what's been going on?" Taiya asked, ready to hear the juice.

"Too damn much," YaYa murmured.

"Well, this thing right here done posted the baby on Facebook and tagged Jay. You know it's been a mess ever since. I also heard KiKi oh wait a minute I mean Keosha, done got all chummy with Endy and 'em," Lynasia counted off.

"Oh, so KiKi rolling with the ops? Fence riding and shit!" Taiya angrily spat.

"Yeah, I told you that hoe is fake as hell. Ain't nothing real about her fake ass," YaYa barked.

"Look, y'all, in her defense, you know she's going to do anything to make CJ happy. If that means rubbing elbows with Endy and Chynna, that's what she's gonna do. You know she loves that man way more than she does us. I'm just being honest," Lynasia said.

"I don't give a damn! I was there for her when her mother was strung out, and she didn't have nowhere to go. I was the one who helped her each time Raymond's old ass whooped her ass and put her out. I was the one there for her when those other mother-fuckers weren't. I went against my kids' father's wishes when it came to the beef with her, Niema, and Endy. I did that shit with no hesitation, Nay!" Taiya yelled.

"Aye, I told you to quiet down. Do you want your visit to end?" yelled Reese the guard again.

"Yo, Taiya, chill out before they make us leave. Damn," YaYa whispered and rubbed her shoulder.

"I know what you're saying, Taiya, but you can't expect people to be like you. KiKi is in love with that dude. We know that now. Look how long it took him to make her his girl? The stupid broad can't even see the bastard only did it because Niema left him to be with Roc. This whole situation is fucking hilarious. It's like everybody within the group messing with each other. It's sad."

Lynasia wanted Taiya to face reality. When it came to Caine, everyone knew Keosha would go with what he wanted her to do. Even if it meant fucking over the people who really loved her. Caine had a hold on her so tight she would cross the people who were there for her the most. Her loyalty was with her man; there was no questioning that. She had fallen deeply for him.

"Well, it won't be long before she and Endy have something in common, because Caine is a dog and arrogant with his shit," joked YaYa to lighten the mood.

"Girl, yes, we all know that. I just don't understand how he gets 'em so hooked,"

Lynasia blurted out loud.

"Y'all know! All jokes aside... Caine is a fine-ass motherfucker," YaYa said, pouting her lips. "I heard dude packing, too! That's what it is. Ain't no way he's taking that chick serious."

"Y'all are so dumb. I'm dead ass about to cry right now," Taiya laughed.

"Well, at least we got you smiling," Lynasia said.

She felt more at ease now that Taiya was enjoying her visit with them.

"My sentencing date is coming up. Whatever happens, just let me know how my babies are doing. I doubt that asshole Rocko will bring them to visit. I know my mom will make sure everything is good I just don't want this bastard to take my kids down South, and they forget all about me," Taiya snarled.

"I don't think he will keep them away from you," Lynasia assured her.

"I hope not, sis. I hope not."

"If he even tried that bullshit, we got you," YaYa told her.

♦ ❤ ♦ RoyaltyCrowned ♦ ❤ ♦

"Are you ready for this trip to Raleigh?" Ari asked Chynna.

"Yeah, I need a getaway, but I wonder why Endy would rather go there than to Florida."

"I don't know. Maybe because she found her husband screwing somebody in Florida. I don't care where we go; I need a break from New York for real, man. Me and Ty have not been getting along at all," Ari admitted.

"What you mean, Ari? What's going on?"

"He's been really distant, sis. We haven't had sex in months. Sometimes he doesn't even come to bed. And when he does, he's always so tired. You know that's not us. We're usually all over each other. I even told Endy about this at Patience's party."

"Girl, I don't think it's that deep. Don't worry yourself too much. He's probably just overworking, and the work he does is manual labor. Really, chick, you have nothing to worry about. Just turn it up a notch in the bedroom on his ass," Chynna advised and winked slyly.

"Okay, I'm not going to worry myself. My mind does wander. I know I talk shit, but I love my husband."

"Ari, don't read too much into it. Just start doing something different. Get rid of the kids for a night or two and spend some quality time together. Ty's not stupid. He loves you and those kids. He wouldn't be disloyal. I don't see it."

"Okay, sis. I hope you're right. I'm going to get rid of the twins. I'm gon' get a room for this weekend––a change of scenery. I got this, sis. Thank you so much. You always know how to make me feel better."

"You know I got you. We will not have no more divorces or breakups. We all have come too far and built way too much. I'll be damned if we gon' let these whores tear down what we built."

"I hear you, boo," Ari said warmly and giggled.

"Okay, now let's get us some fly shit so we can show these girls down South how to get down," Chynna laughed as they walked into Saks.

♦ ♥ ♦ Royalty Crowned ♦ ♥ ♦

"Hey, Endy! What's up? You've been MIA for a minute," Niema spoke into her phone.

"Sorry about that, sis. I've been going back and forth with Jay for the past two weeks. I'm so ready to be in North Carolina."

"Well, I can't wait for y'all to get here either. I need a mommy-free weekend real quick before Reign comes here permanently."

"Are you even ready for that? Girl, it's a lot with two babies. If it wasn't for Ev, Mom-ma, Rizzy, and Jay stepping in, I would be nuts right now," Endy sighed heavily.

"Yeah, but I love my Rocko, so what's his is mine. I'm going to love those girls like I birthed them myself."

"I didn't think y'all two would have made it this far. Sis, if you're happy, I am, too. It took some getting used to, but we're all grown now. I just hope y'all make it for many years to come," Endy expressed sincerely.

"Endy, can I please talk to you before I go?" interrupted Jasean.

"Ny, let me hit you back. Jasean's about to leave."

"Okay, sis, handle your business. Just hit me back later," Niema said and hung up.

"What is it you want to talk about, Jay?" Endy said, her tone cold.

"I miss you, baby. I can't do this. I can't live without y'all, E. I'm sick without you. I miss you so much. I love you, baby. I'm so sorry I hurt you."

"If you loved me, Jay, we wouldn't be going through this. You were thinking with your dick and not with your heart. You have a whole damn baby out there. How am I going to ever be able to live with that?"

Jasean felt like a complete asshole as he watched her shed tears because of him. Once again, he hurt the woman he vowed before God to love and cherish till death do them part. He swore to her after getting caught the first time cheating that he wouldn't do it again. Yet, here they were again because of him.

"I know I can't undo what's done. Endy, I'm willing to do anything for us to get through this. I can't lose you and my kids. Please, E, let me prove It to you."

"Jay, there's no coming back from this. I want a damn divorce! I don't want this mar-riage no more. We can sort out visitation for the kids, but I don't want to spend another moment being married to you!"

Endy started to rush to the bedroom, but Jasean grabbed her forearm and nudged her gently toward him, pressing on her back slightly with his other hand and submerging her in his embrace.

"Baby, you don't mean that. I know you love me, Endy. Please, don't do this."

AFTER THE BETRAYAL

Endy felt the bulge in his pants, and her resolve began to weaken. Her body heated up from being so close to him. It had been a long time since she had sex, and he knew this. He knew exactly what he was doing—what soft spot to strike. Jasean felt her body relax, and he used that opportunity to plant soft kisses on her neck.

"Jay... stop! We're just... not... about to act like nothing happened."

Endy thrust her body backward, trying to resist the throbbing intensity between her legs. Jay could feel her tensing back up, so he began to move his kisses upwards towards her ear.

He licked and nipped at her earlobe until he whispered huskily into her ear, "Baby, don't fight it. I know you want me. I know you want me to be deep inside you, stroking your insides."

Not sensing any resistance from Endy, Jasean slowly walked them back to the couch without stopping his magic touches on her neck and ear—going back and forth and back again. Before Endy could hit the couch, he removed her robe and let it pool at her feet so he could admire her body.

"Wow. Your body is exquisite. I'm a damn fool."

Jasean raised his hand and began fondling Endy's breast. He twirled, pulled, and kneaded her breast just the way she liked. From the expression on her face and the wetness trailing down her thigh, he knew he hadn't lost his touch. Feeling accomplished, Jasean guided her down to the couch and got on his knees to take Endy's exposed breasts into his mouth. Hearing her soft moans excited him, and he wanted to hear more.

"Jayyy... J... J... Jaseannn... Please stop. We can't be doing this right now."

He glanced up at Endy while sucking her breast and said, "Maybe you're right, maybe you're wrong. For now, let's just enjoy this. Let me enjoy your body, and let me enjoy these nuts I'm about to give to you," Jasean murmured while circling the tip of his tongue around her nipples.

He got off the floor and maneuvered his body to hover above her. He kissed the top of her forehead and began a journey down her body while intentionally avoiding the places where she would want to be kissed. When he got to her feet, he sucked on each of her toes while praising how sexy they were. Once every toe received its attention, he slid both his hands down her inner thighs, earning him a shiver and low moan from Endy. He hooked one of her legs over the couch while placing the other over his shoulder and began his descent into her sweet nectar waters.

"Jay, please stop! I can't fall for this bullshit! Or you! I can't... I can't... uh, Jay... uh, uh, uh! God, I love you so much! I missed you! I missed this!" Endy let out the throatiest moan she could muster, succumbing to her sexual needs.

Smiling at her reaction, he kept tasting her until he felt her legs tense up, shake and her hands gripped his hair. His baby was about to cum, and he knew just what she needed to get there. He repositioned his hands to spread her folds to reveal her glistening clit. After a few minutes of suckling and nipping at her clit, Endy came on his tongue. Not wanting to waste a single drop, Jasean slurped her up.

When Jasean stood up, he noticed Endy's eyes were glazed over, and her breathing was a little ragged. He dropped a few feathery kisses on her body in hopes of bringing her back from the stars. Sure enough, she began to hum in response to his kisses. Once he knew she was back, he stepped back and began taking off his clothes.

His manhood was standing at full attention, aching with the desire to be buried within Endy. Jasean approached her and positioned himself at her opening. He rubbed his dick up and down for lubrication to evade hurting her upon entry. Endy squirmed underneath him, but he wasn't budging.

"I can't take it no more," she moaned as she reached down and aligned his manhood at her opening, guiding him into her soaking wet folds.

"Ahh... Damn, baby, I missed being inside you so much!" Jasean moaned loudly.

AFTER THE BETRAYAL

They became in sync with one another, and all felt right in the world again. The more she moaned, the deeper he thrust into her. For that moment, they were lost in the essence; everything they went through was the furthest thing from their mind. They met their climaxes with shouts and grunts of pleasure and folded into one another tiredly as they individually explored the forbidden pleasure that was just given to them. Yet, Endy's pleasure was short-lived, for she was soon in a state of confusion. One part of her regretted their reunion, while the other part of her enjoyed every minute of it.

"I need to get dressed. I got some stuff to do," Endy said nervously as she pushed Jasean off her and jumped up from the couch.

"Babe, come on. Why you rushing to leave?" Jasean questioned as Endy snatched away from his grasp.

"I told you I had something to do, so let me go. I will see you later," she said, growing agitated.

"Okay, babe, I'm sorry. I just missed you, that's all."

"Don't call me babe! Call me Endy. We had a moment; now it's over!" she barked.

"Okay, I won't call you that again. I will do whatever you say. Just please don't leave me," Jasean begged, realizing the sex hadn't changed her mind.

"Boy, bye. Ain't nothing changed. I still want a divorce. I was just horny," Endy scoffed.

Feeling desperate, Jasean grabbed Endy's hands and said, "Yo, you serious, E? I know you still love me. Just say it. Endy, please tell me you still love me."

"Jasean, you are the father of my children, so somewhere inside of me, I still love you. But that doesn't change the fact that I want to divorce you."

"Endy, come on!"

"You said you would do whatever I say. I want a divorce," Endy repeated.

"Endy, come on! No, for real, yo!" replied Jasean, his voice beginning to quiver.

"I am, but thanks for the nut," Endy called back as she walked out of the room.

Jasean sat in shock. He couldn't believe she played him like that, but he knew he deserved it. He wasn't giving up, though. He knew now that he needed to go even harder to win her back.

"You wanna play hard, Endy? Okay, let's play hard. I'm ready for the challenge."

He reached over the couch and picked up his cell phone off the table.

"Yo, CJ! Put the plan in motion. Don't ask no questions. Just do it."

Let's go, Endyia. I'm ready, Jasean thought to himself as he rubbed his hands together.

WHEN A WOMAN'S FED UP

Chapter 8

While the ladies were in North Carolina the following weekend, Caine threw Jasean the biggest welcome-home party. Everybody who was anybody was in attendance. Caine was happy to see his cousin enjoying himself and not worrying about Endy for once. The deejay had the party jumping, and everybody was on the dance floor—until YaYa, Lynasia, and Tiffany walked in.

"Aye! What the hell is she doing here?" shouted Jasean, turning to Caine.

"I don't know. I made sure it was an invite-only event. I'm definitely about to see what's up."

"I'm about to go upstairs to the office. The last thing I need is for somebody to tell Endy that YaYa and me were in the same vicinity," Jasean explained.

He rushed off quickly when he spotted YaYa and her crew making a beeline to him.

"A'ight, I got you, man. Just go 'head," Caine told him as they got closer.

"Why yo' boy run off so quick? I just wanted to say hi and see when he would like to come see Lil' Jay, that's all," YaYa said innocently.

"Sweetheart, I don't know what you did to get in here, but you were not invited,"

Caine barked.

"Boy, bye! This is my baby daddy's welcome home party, isn't it? Why wouldn't I be here?" YaYa retorted.

"Yo, you're mad aggressive right now. I think you need to fall back before you get dragged out of here."

"YaYa, chill," Lynasia intervened, shooting Caine a disapproving look. "I'm pretty sure Jay put them up to this. He has to see you sooner or later. That would be real messed up to put his baby mother out for no reason."

"Yeah, you're right. The bastard can't hide forever. Come on, y'all! Let's go get a drink," YaYa called out.

"These chicks have no respect no more. Yo, keep your eyes out. I'm about to hit the floor and see if there are any other unwanted guests here," Caine told the security guard as he began to make his rounds around the club.

As Caine walked through the club, he saw YaYa talking to the Perez brothers. Caine couldn't help but stare at how sexy YaYa was looking. She wore a short red dress that hugged the shit out of her curves. Her booty was looking phat, her tits nice and perky.

"Girl, look at CJ staring at your ass!" Lynasia mentioned, rolling her eyes. "That dude ain't shit. I don't know why KiKi continues to deal with him. He's a straight hoe."

"You know I know. I told you if I give the bastard some pussy, he will take it, but I ain't even gon' do Jay like that. His ass probably would cry like a baby," giggled YaYa.

"Nah, we not about to do no hoe shit," laughed Lynasia.

"Nah, I'm not gon' do it, sis. That asshole would shit bricks if I gave CJ some coochie, girl."

"Well, good. You know J.J is already mad that I rock with you. Do you...but hell, don't deal with his people."

"Bitch, fuck you."

AFTER THE BETRAYAL

"Yo, Jay said y'all need to go. He doesn't want no problems with Endy," announced Tylon as he walked up to them at the bar.

"Ain't nobody thinking about his ass. I'm just trying to celebrate the fact that my son will have his father in his life," YaYa said.

"Aye, we not on that type of energy tonight. So, either you go by choice...or you go by force."

"Dude, are you serious? It's not that deep. We just came to welcome this bastard home, and he gon' play us like this?!" screamed YaYa in Tylon's face.

"Yo, ma, your best bet is to leave now before shit gets real in here. You're here uninvited. Just take your ass on home and spend time with your son," replied Tylon.

"Motherfucker, I spend time with my son every day. You need to be telling your homeboy that shit!" screamed YaYa even louder.

Security heard the commotion and quickly approached YaYa and her crew to escort them out of the club. If they were going to escort her out of the club, they would have to work for it. YaYa kicked, screamed, and cursed her way through as they dragged her out. Jasean laughed as he watched from the office window.

"Aye, Jay, you got a real problem on your hands with that one. Why the fuck didn't you pull out or tell her to swallow?" Caine joked.

"Because the pussy was good at the time," replied Jasean as he sipped his Henny.

They both looked at each other and busted out laughing. Jasean was over his affair with YaYa. He just wanted his family back at this point and was willing to do anything. The party was jumping, but all Jasean could think about was Endy. He missed her so much that he couldn't even enjoy himself.

"Aye, yo! You and Endy will be back together in no time. Don't sweat that shit! What you need to do is get back to this party, these hoes, and the business," said Caine.

"I know, man. I got to shoot to Philly to talk numbers about opening up the spot there.

I need to get away for a couple of days to clear my mind. Shoot YaYa some cash for the baby, too. I'm leaving in the morning."

"Okay, bet. Yeah, get away. Clear your mind, have some fun, and get you some new pussy," laughed Caine.

"Nah, I'll pass on the new pussy."

"I bet you would. More pussy for me then!" cheesed Caine as he patted Jasean on the shoulder to head back to the party.

"You a straight fool, man."

The two parted ways. Jasean went off to get ready to leave for Philly, and Caine was off to chase women.

♦ ❤ ♦ Royalty Crowned ♦ ❤ ♦

Around six o'clock the next morning, Jasean woke up feeling drained. He only managed to get a few hours of sleep because of his inability to find a comfortable position. He wanted to get to Philadelphia early so he could get back home and check up on the kids. Endy was in North Carolina, and he was worried he was losing her completely.

Ring! Ring! Ring! Ring!

"We need to link... ASAP!" Reeko screeched when Jasean answered his phone.

"What's good, my dude? I'm on my way to Philly to handle some business," replied Jasean.

"Well, you need to get back on the home front. I heard Endy and Chynna over the phone talking about her moving with the kids. That shit true or what?"

"Wait! What?!" Jasean yelled.

"Yeah, my dude. She talking about taking your seeds to North Carolina. I told Chynna, I know the shit you did was fucked up, but don't take the man's kids away --"

"Reeko, thanks for the info," Jasean said, cutting him off. "You know that's not about to go down. She's not about to take my kids no-damn-where. What the hell she thinking? If she wants to go, then she can go, but not my kids! They are staying in New York, period."

"Chill, B. Don't go being all crazy. Just let the shit play out. If you fuck around and approach her the wrong way, you know she gonna be on some bullshit. Just chill in the cut and wait for her to make her move."

"So, you want me to wait until she takes my kids somewhere I don't know about? Fuck no!"

He hung up the phone and started pacing back and forth. After taking a deep breath, he dialed Endy's number.

"Aye, this is Endy of E-Class. Please leave me a message after the tone."

"Oh, so she wants to play games? Let's play. Not answering the phone and shit. Okay, I got you, Endy," he spat, dialing another number.

"Yo, Ma, go by Nana's house and see where my kids at, please. And don't take 'I don't know' as an answer. Somebody knows something," he said.

"Alright, I got you, son. Are you okay?" asked Evelyn.

"Yeah, Ma. I'm good. About to head to Philly for a quick sec to handle some business. I'll be right back."

"Okay, son. Be careful," Evelyn replied.

♦ ♥ ♦ Royalty Crowned ♦ ♥ ♦

Evelyn was ready to put her plan into motion because there was no way she was letting Endy take her grandchildren away from her.

"Hello? I know it's early, Tanya, but can we meet up to talk?"

"It's too damn early, Ev. And I really don't want to get involved in the children's situation. Endy asked me to stay out of it, so I'm trying to respect her wishes."

"I know, Tanya. I get it, but this isn't just about that. Can we please just meet up?"

"Okay. Give me a few hours. We can meet at Ma house," Tanya said, giving in.

"Thanks, Tanya. I just want to find a resolution before things get out of hand," explained Evelyn.

"I feel you, Ev, but Jay brought all this shit on his damn self. He can't blame anyone else."

"I know, but hopefully, we can come up with a resolution when we meet," Evelyn commented, trying to ignore the rude comment about her son.

"Well, I will see you around eleven," said Tanya before hanging up.

"I see this shit is going to go left," murmured Evelyn to herself.

◆ ❤ ◆ RoyaltyCrowned ◆ ❤ ◆

YaYa was getting fed up with Jasean not interacting with her concerning their son or even acknowledging his existence. She tried everything to make him be a part of Lil' Jay's life, but he continued to be distant. Done with trying to be reasonable, she headed to Aunt Sally's house.

"Aunty Sally! It's me, Titi!" YaYa hollered from outside the door. "I need to talk to you, please! I have Lil' Jay with me!"

Aunt Sally sighed before opening the door. She loved YaYa but wasn't in the mood for her nonsense. However, she knew she couldn't just not let her in the house, so she opened the door.

"Come in and take a seat."

"Auntie, I'm sorry. I'm so sorry for everything I have done. I'm sorry for all the pain I have caused everyone. I just want some peace for me and my son. I want him to have his father in his life. That's all, Auntie. That's all I want," cried YaYa as reality began to sink in.

AFTER THE BETRAYAL

"Niyana, baby, I don't even know where to start or what to tell you. You broke up a marriage. You caused pain to someone who did nothing but accept you like family. You hurt Niema in the process! Niema, who did nothing but love and protect you. You acted selfishly, and now you have to reap the consequences of your actions. I'm sorry, baby, but you're going to have to figure this one out on your own. I can't help you, but I do pray you will find peace."

"I don't know what to do, Auntie. I have been praying and praying, but God is not hearing me. I feel like I'm going to snap."

"He hears you, baby. But you can't pray and then turn around and do something evil. Just continue talking to God and ask Him for guidance."

Aunt Sally laid the baby down in his seat so she could console YaYa. She could see she was in a distressed mental state.

"Let God lead you, child. I promise He won't steer you in the wrong direction."

"Auntie, I don't even know where to begin."

"Begin with him, baby. Be there for him," Aunt Sally said as she pointed at Lil' Jay.

Aunt Sally continued to rock her and hum to her until she fell asleep. She then called Niema to see if maybe she could get Endy and YaYa to sit down and come to some type of compromise for the children's sake.

"Hi, Auntie. How you doing?" Niema answered.

"I'm good, baby. How are you, Roc, and Nasim doing?"

"We're great, Auntie. Getting ready to head back up that way to see everyone. I'm happy about that!"

"Well, I don't want to put a damper on your mood, but I did want to talk to you about something," Aunt Sally said reluctantly.

"Talk to me about what, Auntie?"

"It's about your cousin."

"What about her, Aunt Sally?" Niema asked dryly

"Don't sound so excited, Ny."

"Well, I'm sorry if I don't sound excited, but she did come to New York and turn my life upside down for no reason."

"Baby, your cousin is going through it. I'm just a little scared that she might hurt herself, that baby, or even someone else. Jay not accepting the baby is killing her."

"What the hell did she expect, Auntie? He is trying to get back with Endy. He's not about to do anything to piss her off. Besides, YaYa was all cocky when she was doing her shit. I told her that he would make sure the baby was taken care of, but he was not about to be flaunting him in Endy's face. She brought this all on herself, Auntie. I don't feel bad for her. Not one bit."

"I know, Ny. I just wish you and her were in a better place since y'all are blood, that's all. She is really regretting her actions."

"Auntie, I tried with YaYa, but she was so disrespectful and acted like she felt no remorse over the whole situation. I don't even know how to talk to her anymore."

"I understand that, Ny, but she needs help, baby. She needs help!"

"I'm sorry, Aunt Sally. I'm not trying to be disrespectful, but if she doesn't accept her faults in the matter, we will never see eye to eye."

"Life is short, Niema. Please don't hold that grudge forever. I'm going to let you go so you enjoy your family."

"Auntie, I'm sorry. I just don't need that type of stress in my life right now."

"Okay, baby. I hate to have bothered you. I'll let you go. I have to make the baby a bottle. I love you, Niema...and I pray you girls make amends."

"Talk to you later, Auntie," Niema replied.

AFTER THE BETRAYAL

"Who was that?" Rocko asked, seeing the expression on Niema's face.

"Aunt Sally wants me to have a conversation with my cousin."

Rocko frowned. "Have a conversation about what?"

"She is still my family, Roc. Believe me, I don't like none of this shit either, but I eventually will have to talk to her about this whole situation. I just know that right now, I'm not in the mood to do it."

"Well, I'm definitely not fucking with her. That hot shit she pulled with Jay was trifling. She got mad motherfuckers involved that had nothing to do with that shit. My family welcomed her with open arms, and this is what she does," Rocko replied, getting angry all over again.

"I get it, boo. Really, I do. But you have to understand that's still my blood. At some point, I'm going to have to forgive her and move past this. Endy knows I love her, but she also knows I love my cousin, too."

"I'm never dealing with her like that. She did some ol' hoe shit, and that's never gonna be forgiven by me."

"I understand, Roc. I would never force you to talk to her, but I want you to understand I'm caught in the middle."

"I know, baby. I just hate she took shit as far as to have a baby by that dude. He's a clown for even playing my cousin like that, knowing we all like family."

"Oh, shoot! Endy posted something," Niema said, opening her Facebook to a pic of Jasean with Patience and Peace.

"What is it?" Rocko asked.

"It's a pic of Jay with the kids. They look like they're at your nana's house."

"What! I know she ain't taking that clown back!" Rocko barked, dialing on his phone.

"Roc, that girl is grown. You can't tell her what to do. At the end of the day, they are married. You better mind your business," spazzed Niema.

"Forget that shit. This clown cheated and got another broad pregnant. That shit ain't cool," Rocko yelled and waited for Endy to answer. "Yo, cuz! What's going on? What's with posting Jay and shit?"

"Well, hello to you, too. He is my kids' father. Why wouldn't I post him with them?" replied Endy calmly.

"The dude is foul as hell! You need to take that bullshit down!" demanded Rocko.

"Sir, I'm gonna need you to pipe down. I'm grown. You need to calm your ass down and worry about your own shit. Believe it or not, I have a new man anyway, honey. Now, like I said, he is my kids' father, and we are on cordial terms. I'm not trying to beef with that man. Plus, I can post whatever the hell I want."

"Damn, my bad, cuz. I just hate how the asshole did you, man. I know you deserve better. I'll see you soon."

"I get it, cuz, but I'm trying to co-parent the best way I know how," explained Endy.

"She told you to mind your business, huh?" laughed Niema.

"Alright, cuz. I love you. See you soon," Rocko said, then he hung up.

"She got you, didn't she?" Niema chuckled.

"What does she mean she got a new man?" questioned Rocko.

"Exactly what she said. He's a cutie, too," smiled Niema.

Niema's phone rang. It was Aunt Sally again.

"What? Lord have mercy! Auntie, please calm down. She will be okay. I will be up there as soon as I can," Niema stated as she tried to calm her aunt down.

"Yo, yo, yo! What's going on?" Rocko asked nervously, his eyes bulging out of their sockets.

"YaYa saw the picture Endy posted of Jay and the kids. She went crazy and left the baby with Aunt Sally."

"She's really bugging about a man that isn't her man. Tell Auntie she probably doesn't need to have Lil' Jay with her right now anyway."

"Auntie, please calm down. She will be alright. This is what she has to go through because of her actions," remarked Niema.

Aunt Sally hung up so she could tend to the baby. Niema reached out to YaYa but received no response, so she tried again via text.

"YaYa, I know we haven't been seeing eye to eye, but just know I do still love you. If you need me, call me. We are still family."

"Baby, don't worry. It's going to be okay. YaYa's just going through the motions right now. Hopefully, all this shit will blow over soon. I'm sorry, ma. I know you hate being in the middle," Rocko said as he cradled Niema.

"I just want it all to go away!" Niema whined.

"Maybe Jay and YaYa will work things out and raise their son. If I know my cousin, she won't be getting back with Jay. When a woman reaches the last straw, there's no chance of winning her back."

KNUCK IF YOU BUCK

Chapter 9

Endy rolled over and patted around her nightstand in search of her vibrating phone. What the hell does my mom want now? she thought when she saw Tanya's name on the screen.

"Endyia!" Tanya hollered.

"Ma, please, stop. It's too early for all that yelling. What's going on?"

"Why is Ev trying to meet up again? What's going on now?"

"Momma, I told you to stop answering her. Jay and I are cool, so I don't know what her agenda is. She's just upset because I've been ignoring her calls. I told her she could see the kids whenever she wants. I just need my space. She wanted us to continue acting like family, but I'm not up for it."

"Well, you and Ev need to figure out what y'all going to do and dead this mess. Fix this shit ASAP!" yelled Tanya into Endy's ear before hanging up.

Lord, why don't these people leave me alone? I just want to move on with my life! I'm so ready to go back to North Carolina already.

Endy shook her head as she dialed Jasean's number.

AFTER THE BETRAYAL

"Yo, where you at with my kids, E? It's been two weeks, man," barked Jasean as soon as he answered.

"Dude, I didn't call you to argue. Meet me at my nana's house so we can lay all this shit on the table. The kids are with me. Tell Ma Ev so she can see them, too. I told y'all to get the kids when y'all want, but I don't have to be a part of it," Endy responded calmly, not allowing Jasean to get to her.

"Baby, I'm sorry. I just miss y'all, man! I want my family back," Jasean mumbled.

"Whatever, Jay. Meet me there," Endy said and hung up.

Although this situation was far from over, Jasean was glad Endy agreed to meet with him. He knew it would take a lot of making up, but he was willing to put in the work. Losing his family was not an option.

I'm going to do whatever it takes to get my wife and my kids back home, he thought and smiled hopefully.

"Mr. Newman, are you ready to head back to New York now?" the driver asked him.

"Yeah, I'm ready. I need to go to Brooklyn really quick, though," he said, hopping in the Escalade.

◆ ♥ ◆ RoyaltyCrowned ◆ ♥ ◆

Everyone arrived at Luella's house within the next hour. When Jasean first got there, he tried to act cold and distant; however, he wanted to jump for joy when he saw Endy and the kids. Endy stretched out on the chaise, exhausted from everything. She watched as he interacted with the kids, grinning from ear to ear at his babies. He had missed them so much and would give anything in the world to have his family back. Tanya sat on the sofa and watched as Jasean and Evelyn enjoyed the babies. Meanwhile, Luella was in the kitchen cleaning up.

Tanya cleared her throat to get everyone's attention. "I need everyone to sit down so we can come to a resolution."

"I don't see why we need a resolution. My decision is to file for a divorce, and we co-parent. What's so hard about that?" interrupted Endy.

"See what I'm talking about? She has no consideration for the kids' needs right now," griped Jasean.

"No, it's you that didn't have no consideration for your kids' needs! You're the one who cheated and had another baby!" screamed Endy.

"Endy, calm down and sit your ass down. We're not doing this today. You are being very disrespectful. I understand you're upset, but speak without being vulgar," retorted Tanya.

"I'm sorry, Mommy. I just don't see the point of this meeting. I want a divorce, and that's it. I will never take the kids from them, but we're done. I love you, Ma Ev, but the shopping and dinners are too much. I want to move on with my life," reiterated Endy.

"Jasean, what do you have to say?" Luella asked, looking over at him.

"What can I say? She made up her mind. She doesn't want to work it out, so I will give her what she wants," replied Jasean sadly.

"Motherfucker, I know you're not sitting here sulking. I have tried to be cordial with your sorry ass, but it's just not enough!" yelled Endy again.

"If you keep on cursing and hollering, I'm going to smack the hell out of you. Now stop acting like a gutter rat and act like a grown woman," snapped Tanya.

Endy humbled herself and sat down.

"I'm sorry, Ma. You're right. I'm above this bullshit. So, let's do this... we can set a schedule for the kids and go from there. I think I'm being completely fair. Y'all seeing the kids shouldn't consist of me being there."

AFTER THE BETRAYAL

"Endy, I miss you and our time together, but I guess I will have to get used to not having that anymore. I love you and my grandkids to death. I hope you know that," said Evelyn.

"First, I want to apologize for my disrespect, Ma Ev. You know I love you very much. We've always had a special bond. Y'all just don't know how much this whole situation has hurt me to my core. I just want to get a divorce, co-parent, and move on with my life."

Endy had said her peace. It was the first time she showed any real emotion since the day it happened. That immediately broke Jasean down. Everyone in the room fell silent except for Tanya, who held her baby girl while telling her it was going to be okay. Evelyn's heart was breaking by the moment. She knew how much they loved each other, but she also knew how much pain Jasean had caused.

"Jasean, you need to say something." Evelyn nudged her son, but he was stuck.

"Baby, I'm sorry! I fucked up. I really fucked up!" Jasean cried as he fell to his knees, cradling his face.

Endy had never seen Jasean like that before; his reaction immediately calmed her down, but she found herself feeling pity for him rather than affection. She walked over to him and knelt to hug him.

When he got himself together and noticed it was Endy hugging him, he cried even harder. This made Endy start crying again, and they began to cry in each other's arms.

"I'll get it," Luella announced upon hearing a gentle knock on the door.

Luella opened the door to find YaYa with her right arm arrogantly stretched across the sidelight.

"YaYa, what the hell are you doing here?"

"Nana, I'm not here for any trouble. I heard Jay was here with the kids and felt like this would be a good time for me to talk with him and Endy. I don't care what y'all think about me, but my son and Endy's children share the same father, and nothing will change that. I just want peace and a chance to apologize."

"Child, do you have a death wish? Why would you come here after all the chaos you've caused? If you don't get your ass away from here," raged Luella.

YaYa tried to explain herself again, but she was only able to get out three words before Endy came charging outside.

"Endy, no!" shouted Luella as she tried to restrain Endy, but it was too late.

YaYa and Endy began rolling and fighting on the porch. Endy had been waiting for this moment since she found YaYa and Jay having sex in Miami. When everyone heard the commotion, they came running to the front door. Jasean raced over to the two women and grabbed Endy while Evelyn grabbed YaYa.

"What the hell are you doing here?" rebuked Evelyn as she snatched YaYa by the arm.

"I'm sick of everybody acting like my baby's not shit! He's a part of this family, too!" she screamed while crying.

"Fuck you, YaYa! Do you really think I care about you or that bastard baby of yours?" Endy screamed back.

"E, chill out. You're bigger than this," said Jasean.

"Child, please go ahead home!" Luella yelled as she pulled a bloody-nosed YaYa away from the house.

Meanwhile, Tanya dragged a disheveled Endy back to the living room to calm her down. Jasean hated what he had done to his wife. To see her so hurt, broken, and angry made him feel less than a man. He wished he could rewind time and go back to all the times he fucked up so Endy wouldn't hurt—especially that night.

"Fuck you, Jay! I'm dealing with all this nonsense because of your trifling ass. I'm fighting bitches because of you. I'm divorcing your ass because of your actions, not mine. If you wanted to break me down, you succeeded! You happy now?" Endy ran away sobbing.

"Baby, I'm sorry!" yelled Jasean.

"That's not enough, Jay. You have to do something," Evelyn said firmly. "If I lose my grandchildren over your nonsense, you can forget about me, too."

"Ma, what do you want me to do? I can't make her take me back!"

"Who the hell you think you talking to? You created this bed, so lay in it. You can't blame no one but yourself for this fuck up."

"Okay, y'all, we got to stay levelheaded. We can't all go at each other's throats. I understand the concern, but North Carolina is not across the country. Now, if this is what she needs to do to get past the pain and start over, you have to respect it. The only thing you can do is make sure y'all work something out so you can see the children as much as possible, but you owe her that much," Luella said matter-of-factly.

"You're right, Nana. I just don't know what I'm going to do without them. How can I live without my family? Endy's my rib, y'all. How am I gonna live without her?" Jasean asked rhetorically, gazing blankly around the room.

"Well, son, you have to figure that out. I guess we're done here, so I'm gonna check on my grandbaby. I really hope y'all can come to some type of common ground. Right now, just give her time and space," said Luella as she hugged Evelyn and Jasean goodbye.

"Yes, we will let her have some space. I love y'all, and thanks for everything," Evelyn said.

After they left, Tanya tried to keep the children calm while Luella went to check on Endy. Luella followed the sound of Endy's crying and walked over to comfort her.

"Go 'head and let it out, baby girl," she whispered and sat next to her.

"Nana, I tried not to get out of character, but that hoe kept trying me!"

Endy embraced her grandmother and let the tears flow.

"It's okay, baby. You know I would have done the same damn thing...if not worse. I probably would have shot somebody. Y'all got tempers just like me. It's a blessing and a curse sometimes." Luella chuckled as she reminisced on her past encounters.

"I just want to get this divorce and move to North Carolina. I love New York, but I can't be here with him while he takes care of another child. I'm ready to move on with my life."

"Are you sure that's what you want, baby?"

"Yeah, Nana. I will never trust him again. Plus, I met someone, so I want to give it a fair chance. And I'm going to get tired of beating YaYa's ass," Endy murmured humorously and winked.

"You did whoop her good, too. That's what she gets for messing with my baby. Who comes to the Hinton's house thinking you gon' talk shit and not wear an ass whipping? Where they do that at?" laughed Luella, shaking her head.

"Nana, you crazy. I love you so much. Can you just tell them to leave, please?"

"They're already gone, baby. I told them to give you some time to cool off."

"Thanks, Nana. I'm completely done with Jay, but I will always love Ma Ev."

"Evelyn knows that, baby."

◆ ❤ ◆ RoyaltyCrowned ◆ ❤ ◆

"Girl, what happened to you? Why is there blood on your shirt?" Lynasia asked YaYa when she saw her bloody shirt and messy hair.

"Me and your wack-ass cousin-in-law just got into a fight at Nana's house!"

Lynasia looked at her like she was crazy.

"What the fuck? Why did you go over there when you knew Endy was there?"

"Because I'm tired of them acting like Lil' Jay doesn't exist!"

At this point, YaYa sounded like a broken record, repeating the same painful chords over and over again.

"YaYa, no matter how you see it, you were in the wrong, period," Lynasia stated.

"Okay, but what about Jay? He was wrong, too! Why is nobody upset with him? Why is everyone blaming me?!"

"He's not excused, but at the end of the day, that is that girl's husband. Yeah, I don't deal with J.J.'s family like that, but what you did was wrong, baby. So now you have to face the music."

"I get it, Nay. Damn. What about my son? He needs his father, too. He needs to step up and be a man. Money doesn't replace time," YaYa whined.

Lynasia walked over and hugged her.

"Nay, I know I was wrong. Deadass wrong, but damn, the baby is innocent. He knew what could happen when we laid down together."

"Well, it's time to fight fire with fire. You got to deal with them Hintons on another level and with discretion. You can't go in barking all the time, YaYa. That's not going to work. Just humble yourself and let things play out. You can't force Jasean to be in that baby's life."

"I'm going to try it your way because obviously, Endy's not going to budge. I do, however, owe my cousin a sincere apology. She didn't have anything to do with this," YaYa admitted, wiped her face, and got herself together.

"Yeah, even though I don't fuck with Ny like that, she didn't deserve to be put in the middle. Hell, she got enough to worry about with her own situation. I don't see how everyone feels what she did is okay. She was dead wrong, too," Lynasia acknowledged.

"Yeah, but of course, the excuse is Taiya cheated on Roc first, so it's different. I'm not gon' sweat it. They are supposed to be in town this week to get Taiya's girls, so I will talk to her then. Right now, I need to get back to Aunt Sally's. I know she's waiting to curse me out."

"Just remember what I told you; humble yourself. Let this shit play out," Lynasia said as they made their way to the door.

They were startled to see Keosha standing there motionless.

"What's good, baby?" Keosha asked with a wide grin, Cadence swinging in her arms.

"Bitch, I know you didn't bring your ass here after setting up YaYa and ducking us for weeks," retorted Lynasia.

"Look, I know y'all mad at me. I just want peace at this point in my life. I thought maybe she and Ev could work something out," Keosha explained.

"PEACE?! Bitch, you straight set me up and betrayed us for them. What the hell you talking about?" replied YaYa, jumping in Keosha's face.

"First of all, it wasn't like that. Ev knew I could get you to come. She told me it was to talk and see Lil' Jay. I fell for it, not knowing what she was up to. At this point, I'm just trying to protect Cadence."

"What about you being all buddy-buddy with the Hintons?" asked Lynasia.

"Aye yo, I didn't come over to be asked fifty questions. I came to see if we could salvage our relationship, Lynasia. YaYa, you're not my friend, so I don't owe you shit!"

"Hoe, get the hell away from my door—you and your slipup baby. How you going to come apologize and talk shit at the same time?" Lynasia scoffed.

Keosha's eyes filled with tears, and she held Cadence a little tighter.

"Slip up?! Are you freaking serious right now, Nay? You're mad because I don't want to do this kiddie rivalry shit with you no more?"

"Damn right. You're a disloyal hoe. Get the hell on. Don't contact me at all from now on!" Lynasia screamed an inch away from Koesha's face.

"Nay, don't do it. She has her baby with her," YaYa insisted as she pulled Lynasia back to the entryway.

"This hoe better step then! You're not welcome here no more! Our friendship is done!" Lynasia continued screaming.

"I got you, Nay. Just because I'm not with the drama and grew the fuck up, you're mad! Wow! I got something for both y'all bitches!"

AFTER THE BETRAYAL

SUICIDE

Chapter 10

"**B**abe, your cousin is nuts, man!" Rocko yelled on the phone.

"What's the matter? What happened now?" Niema responded impatiently.

"She's in a rage. YaYa and Endy got to fighting here at Ma's house."

"What, babe? Are you serious? I'm about to have a straight-up talk with this chick because she's overdoing it!"

"Yeah, disrespecting my grandma in her house definitely was not the move."

"I know, baby. I got this. I will call you back once I'm on the way. I just got to Aunt Sally's," Niema said before hanging up.

When Aunt Sally opened up the door, she rejoiced at the sight of Niema.

"Hi, baby! I'm so happy to see you!"

They gave each other a hug and made their way into the house.

"It's good to see you, too. Aunt Sally, where's YaYa?" Niema asked.

"She's in the room upstairs. Go on up and make amends."

"Auntie, did you know your niece went to Nana's house and fought Endy? She's doing way too much at this point."

Aunt Sally shook her head in disappointment.

"YAYA!" Niema screamed as she made her way upstairs.

She was met with no response.

"Niyana Bradley! I know you heard me calling you!" Niema screamed louder as she neared YaYa's bedroom.

When Niema opened the door, she couldn't believe what she saw—a passed-out YaYa with pills sprawled out on the floor, and the baby whimpering in his car seat.

"Auntie! Call 911!"

Aunt Sally jumped up from the couch and rushed upstairs.

"Oh, no, Ny! What happened?"

"I don't know! I came up here, and this is how I found her. She was passed out and unresponsive with the pill bottle beside her!" Niema cried hysterically.

"You go call 911 while I do CPR on her!"

Fifteen minutes later, the paramedics arrived and YaYa was rushed to New York Community Hospital. Niema called Rocko and told him to meet them there.

"YaYa, please don't give up. I love you, cousin," Niema sobbed and then gazed upwards. "Please, God, let her be okay!"

She jumped in her car and followed the ambulance at full-speed, her tears clouding her vision and rendering her driving erratic.

"Calm down, baby," Aunt Sally pleaded as she held the edges of her seat tightly.

They met Rocko, Luella, and Karishma at the hospital.

Rocko rushed to Niema and squeezed her, trying to hug her pain away.

"Baby, what happened?!"

"We found YaYa unconscious on the floor with a note on Lil' Jay that said she lost everything and her baby will never know his father. I don't want my cousin to die!" sobbed

AFTER THE BETRAYAL

Niema into his chest.

"Babe, I don't want that either. I'm praying she pulls through."

"I feel like shit, Roc. She tried to reach out to me. She tried to talk to me, but I let my stubbornness get in the way. God, please let her make it... please!"

♦ ❤ ♦ RoyaltyCrowned ♦ ❤ ♦

When Endy was informed about YaYa's misfortune, she wanted to feel sorry for her but couldn't get over her own pain to do so.

"Who was that?" asked Tanya.

"That was Nana. She said YaYa was found unconscious, and they had to rush her to the hospital. It looked like she tried to commit suicide."

Endy said it so casually that it almost frightened Tanya about how she responded to the situation.

"Well, I know Ny is at the hospital. Do you mind driving me there? I just can't do it alone right now. Aunt Sally must be a nervous wreck. I'll go but only for them," Endy said with a sigh.

Tanya hugged her daughter because she knew it took a lot to make that decision.

"That's what I'm talking about, baby," she said proudly.

They were at Brooklyn Hospital in less than an hour. They arrived to find a screaming, close-to-fainting Aunt Sally and a desperate Luella trying to hold her balance.

Endy's stomach dropped for a minute until she heard her Nana say, "She's okay, Sally. She's going to be just fine."

Endy breathed a sigh of relief. She thought YaYa was gone.

Niema spotted Endy and raced to her best friend for a hug. She knew the hospital was the last place Endy wanted to be, but she was glad to see her.

"How's she doing, Ny?" asked Endy.

"She's stable, but she's not completely in the clear. They had to work on her for an hour. I'm just praying God sees her through this," cried Niema.

"In spite of everything, I would never want this. Sis, hear me when I say that I'm here for you fully," assured Endy.

The moment came when she finally saw Lil' Jay for the first time. She couldn't help but melt because she loved children. He favored Jasean and her children so much that she couldn't deny it. He was so gorgeous with his almond-colored complexion and jet-black curly hair. He was an innocent baby, a bundle of purity. How could I dislike something so precious? she thought.

"Thanks, E. I love you so much; I swear I do."

After sitting in the ICU family waiting room for about forty-five minutes, Endy decided to do the one thing she didn't want to do—but she knew she needed to do. She texted Jasean the bad news.

Jay, I just thought you should know that YaYa is in the hospital for attempted suicide. I know things aren't the best, but I would appreciate it if you would come here for moral support and to see Lil 'Jay. At the end of the day, she is your son's mother. We're at Brooklyn Hospital.

"Lord, Sally is a nervous wreck!" Luella said, exasperated as she walked up on Endy.

"It's to be expected. This is so unfortunate. How is she doing?"

"She's going to be okay. Her throat is going to be a little sore. I came over here to let you know I'm proud of you for being the bigger person. Sometimes we got to put our feelings aside for the people we love. I just hate that you're having to face all this. This will be your testimony, baby girl," remarked Luella.

"I'm good, Nana. I got plans for my babies and me. The divorce should be final soon.

and I can finally move on with my life. By the way, I texted Jay and let him know so he can at least be here for his son."

"Well, that was big of you, baby. He does need to be here. I hope that in regards to the divorce, you're taking everything into consideration--even down to being a single mom because it is a lot of work. I just want you to be sure about your decision."

Endy kissed her cheek and walked away before turning around and stating, "I'm very sure, Nana. I promise you that. I made sure the kids and I will be okay without him."

♦ ❤ ♦ RoyaltyCrowned ♦ ❤ ♦

"Yo, Momma! Endy just texted me to go to the ER. Something about YaYa trying to commit suicide and Lil' Jay there," sputtered Jasean, beginning to panic.

"Jay, calm down. Damn! Call her and see exactly what's going on."

"What? Fuck that! I'm going down there. What if my son was there with her? I told you her ass too unstable to raise him," Jasean barked.

"Just call Endy and see what's going on," Evelyn told him. "You can't just leave, asshole! You're on curfew with an ankle monitor. Stop acting like a damn fool and think!"

"A'ight, a'ight!" he said as he picked up his phone to call Endy.

"Well, did she say what happened?" asked Evelyn.

"What?! I don't care about that shit! Where's my son?" screamed Jasean on the phone.

"Jay, what the hell is going on?" answered a bewildered Endy.

"Sorry about that... was talking to my mother. I'm just worried about the baby. Thanks for telling me, but I can't come up there right now. I'm calling my lawyer and the bails bondsman now. Ma should be there soon, though. Thank again, babe," Jasean said before hanging up.

"Okay, what the hell is going on, Jay? And what do you mean I should be there soon?"

"Well, Ma, I think this is my way out! I got a plan."

"What you mean your way out? What plan?" questioned Evelyn.

"Ma, I need you to go pick up Lil' Jay from Brooklyn Hospital."

"What? Sally's not letting me get that child."

"Ma, just listen to me. She's not stable. I have to get my son! He's your grandchild, too...no matter how he got here."

"Okay, okay, Jay... I know that! I just hate all this chaos going on."

♦ ❤ ♦ RoyaltyCrowned ♦ ❤ ♦

"Greetings. Is this the family of Niyana Bradley?" asked a woman with a police officer at her side.

Niema looked them up and down and finally said, "Who's asking?"

"I'm Casandra Whitley, a social worker with ACS, and we got a report of child neglect for infant Jasean Newman Jr.," stated Ms. Whitley as she gave Niema her credentials.

Aunt Sally was midway to Niema when she caught the last part of Ms. Whitley's introduction.

"I know damn well y'all are not here to take her child!" Aunt Sally cried out. "She's just going through postpartum depression. I'm sure you can understand that!"

"Ma'am, I completely understand, but when something like this is reported, we have no choice but to follow up on it. The baby will be placed with the next of kin," Ms. Whitley explained.

"We are his next of kin!" Niema spoke up.

93

AFTER THE BETRAYAL

"And so are we!" stated Evelyn as she walked up and stood beside Ms. Whitley.

"Evelyn, you know damn well none of y'all want no dealings with this baby. Why are y'all doing this?" cried Aunt Sally.

"The same reason your niece brought her ass here and turned everybody's world upside down. Because we feel like it."

"You're a spiteful bitch!" replied Aunt Sally as she lunged at her.

"Hold up, Sally! Y'all don't do this here," stated Luella, grabbing Aunt Sally's arm.

The officer moved to stand between Sally and Evelyn. He then cleared his throat and turned to Niema.

"Ma'am. Please give the baby to Ms. Whitley," instructed the officer.

"Okay, fine!"

Niema walked back to the waiting area and grabbed the car seat holding Lil' Jasean. When she returned and handed over her cousin's son, Ms. Whitley gave Niema some paperwork with follow-up questions in return.

Endy shot Evelyn a disapproving look on her way out... Who uses a suicide attempt as a means to take a baby?

LOCKED UP

Chapter 11

"Why are you here after that little stunt you pulled the other day?" Niema growled at Evelyn, who was waiting outside for her on the porch.

"I need to talk to Endy. Do you know where she is?"

Evelyn aggressively pushed past Niema into the house.

"Evelyn, what is it now, huh? You have some nerve barging into my house like this," Luella threatened.

Evelyn stopped walking around and turned to them. "I think y'all need to hear me out first."

Niema remained silent, her arms crossed in defiance

"It seems Jay's case done got really serious," Evelyn continued.

"What do you mean, serious? I hope they don't mess with my grandchild behind his nonsense!"

"She needs to put everything in someone else's name. The feds are coming for everything...even E-Class," explained Evelyn.

AFTER THE BETRAYAL

"What? Why? She used her savings and credit to get that store. Why would they come after her stuff?" questioned Luella.

"Well, since they are still legally married, they're coming after her assets, as well. She's a good girl and doesn't deserve none of this."

"Lord have mercy. What is my grandbaby going to do? She doesn't deserve to lose all that she has worked so hard for. Your son chose to continue to live like he was in the streets instead of turning all the way legit!" Luella stated bitterly.

"Nana, calm down. Now we know Endy got to have a plan. She's smart. So, I know damn well she's not taking this shit lying down."

Luella instinctively shot her an evil look but then softened at the realization that Evelyn was looking out for Endy.

"You're right, Ny! I'm going to wait for Endy to get back here. We need to let her know what's going on."

♦ ❤ ♦ RoyaltyCrowned ♦ ❤ ♦

"Aye, why is Endy going down South so much? And why y'all always here running her businesses?" Tanya asked Karishma and Chynna.

"Auntie, your guess is as good as mine. I really couldn't tell you for real. Knowing Endy, it has to be something involving money." Chynna shrugged. "I wish she would tell us so we can help her. She's been so distant lately."

"I feel like she is planning her next move."

"If she does go to North Carolina, I want to go, too. I'm tired of New York," Chynna muttered.

"Shit, I don't! It's too slow and country down there. I just hope she continues to let me run the store," laughed Karishma.

"Slow is not always bad. The cost of living is cheaper. They have big houses with backyards for kids. I don't know how Reeko would feel about moving that far, though," responded Chynna.

"I'm a true New Yorker. I have no desire to move down South. If that's what Endy wants to do, more power to her. I just hope she's not letting YaYa and Jay run her away. Running never solves anything!" remarked Tanya.

"I don't think it's that, Auntie. Sometimes you just need a new environment...a new atmosphere," said Chynna.

"What's up, ladies!" announced Jay as he entered Endy's store.

Chynna looked him up and down before walking away.

"Damn, it's like that, Chy?" Jay chuckled.

"Dude, don't play with me! What the hell do you want? Endy isn't here."

"He's here for me. I asked him to come by so we can talk. Arguing and being upset is not getting us anywhere," stated Tanya.

"I'm not at that point yet, so I'm leaving. Can you watch the spot, Chynna?" Karishma asked.

"Be back in an hour, chick. I'm going to check the inventory while you're gone so they can talk!" Chynna yelled as Karishma walked out the door.

Tanya turned to Jay. "Okay, are you ready to talk, Mr. Newman?"

"Yes, let's talk."

They headed to Endy's office and sat down.

"You do know your marriage is over, right?"

"Yeah, I know. I tried everything to let Endy know I'm sorry, but she's not budging at all, Ma. I don't know what else to do but give her what she wants."

"What did you expect to happen? Now I have a question for you. Did y'all have anything to do with YaYa getting fired from her job?"

"I'm not going to confirm or deny that. What I do know is that I've told her too many times to stop trying to ruin my marriage and do right by my son. I guess she got what was coming to her," Jasean said sternly.

"Okay, whatever. I need you to make sure Endy does not go down for your bullshit. My daughter has been through enough."

"Ma, I get it. I just need Endy to be fair and honest with me. I'm not going for my kids leaving New York. I'm on probation and may be getting some time. I can't leave the state, and she knows that. Please tell her not to take my kids away. They're all I got."

"I will see what I can do, Jay, but I can't make no promises. Endy is a grown woman. If going away brings her peace, then so be it."

The office door flew open. It was Karishma with a worried look on her face.

"Girl, what's wrong with you? Why you come rushing in here like that?" Tanya asked.

"Hmm, I need to talk to you about something important."

"I need to get out of here anyway. So, can I come pick up the kids later? I will take them back to Nana's house later on tonight."

"Yeah, that's cool. I'll get them once I'm done shopping. We will talk more later," replied Tanya as she walked Jasean out of the office, ready to see what was going on with Karishma.

"OKAY, CHYNNA! COME ON!" shouted Karishma to the back.

"Dang, I said I was coming, little girl. What's so important you need to tell us?"

"Y'all are not going to believe what I just saw," began Karishma.

"What? What is it, girl?!"

"I just saw Caine and YaYa's ass together uptown. It didn't look very cordial either. They looked a little too friendly and close to me."

"What? Hell no! Are you sure, Rizzy? Aunt Sally was talking like Yaya had learned her lesson and wanted to do right so she can get Lil' Jay back. Why would she deal with Caine? There has to be a logical explanation."

Chynna was hoping Karishma was mistaken. The last thing Niema needed to hear right now was that her cousin was back on that bullshit train.

Karishma pulled out her phone and thrust it in the air.

"Look at this."

Sure enough, it was a video of Caine and YaYa together.

Tanya took a peek at the phone and said, "Lord, we need to get to Jay before he finds out another way. YaYa is really on some savage bullshit these days."

ANTE UP

Chapter 12

"**E**ndy, have you made a decision yet? This is a great deal my boss gave you," asked Thee as they both stood in front of this exquisite house in North Carolina.

"Hmm, the area is nice, but I just don't know yet! I'm still debating. I haven't even told Jay I'm moving yet."

"Girl, it's time you live for you. Your kids should be your only priority. Jay should have no say-so over if you move or not. You can't live your life according to others' opinions and feelings. Besides, I think Mr. Richmond would really like for you to come on down here," Thee teased and giggled.

Endy's phone vibrated, and she saw she had a message from her mother.

When exactly are you getting back? Jay is fishing around trying to find out what you are doing. You need to let him know you're thinking about moving down South soon!

Endy rolled her eyes, preparing to shut the phone off until another message from her mother came through.

Meet me at Momma's house as soon as you land. We need to talk.

"There's some shit going on. I have to get ready to go. I will be in touch real soon, cousin," said Endy as she walked toward her rental.

"Endy, just remember, it's time for you to live for you and the kids. You got a promising future here in North Carolina. Don't sleep on it," Thee insisted.

"I know, cuz. I'm telling you I'm definitely leaving New York. I just have to let Jay know so he can be prepared, that's all."

After Endy got back to Aunt Linda's house and packed her things up, she headed straight to Raleigh-Durham Airport for her flight. When her flight arrived at JFK Airport, she called Chynna to see what was going on.

"Where the hell are you, E?" said Chynna when she picked up the call.

"I just got to the airport and need to go to Nana's house. Are you still picking me up? What's going on? My mom called me, and she sounded upset."

"I'm on my way right now. Girl, she's upset because we found out the feds are picking up Jay's case. Ev said they may be going after your business and assets. Then Evelyn or Jay got YaYa fired from her job. And to top it off, Rizzy saw Caine and YaYa getting real cozy!" Chynna said, bringing her cousin up to speed.

"What?! I'll be there soon."

What the hell is going on with these people? Endy thought as she ended the call.

◆ ❤ ◆ RoyaltyCrowned ◆ ❤ ◆

Endy arrived at her grandmother's house, and once she settled in, she began asking the important questions.

"What the hell is going on?! I thought Keosha and YaYa were cool? Why is she out and about with Caine?!"

"Girl, my damn cousin is back at it again. I think she found out that KiKi was the one bringing us info, and now she's mad. So, I guess she's trying to play get-back."

"How the hell would she know that?" asked Endy.

"I don't know, but you would think that by her almost losing her life, she would sit her ass down somewhere—especially since she lost her job. But no, she wants to run around causing chaos," Niema fumed while pacing the room.

"Would you sit the hell down? You makin' my nerves bad, Ny," Endy chuckled.

Niema stopped pacing and smirked.

"Hey, I think I got a way to make YaYa go back to New Orleans so we can finally have some peace."

"How?" Rocko asked curiously, his eyes lighting up.

"We're gonna tell Keosha and Marilyn about her and Caine if she doesn't. You know once Marilyn gets a hold of this information, she's gon' flip. You know she ain't taking no chances of losing her grandbaby," Niema said.

"Okay, so now that's cleared up. What are they saying about Jay?" asked Endy.

"Well, it seems they are going after all his assets—yours included. You need to file for a divorce ASAP, and I mean like yesterday," said Niema.

"Honey, I did that a few weeks ago. I just hadn't said anything. He actually granted it to me with no problem. Now I see why."

"Chick, what? You mean to tell me I was worried, and y'all already divorced?"

"I know how you feel, but we had to keep it quiet. He had a feeling the feds would pick up his case."

"Okay, so what you have in mind for YaYa? She and the Newmans are crazy as hell. You have to go at them the right way," Rocko said to Niema.

"I know, babe. I'm not stupid."

"Well, if we gonna do this shit, we need to plan it carefully! You know Caine can get really dirty. I don't want it to be a big mess," stated Endy.

Just then, someone knocked on the door.

"Who is that?" Endy whispered suspiciously.

"It's Keosha," Rocko called out when he looked through the peephole.

"I called her, boy. Now let her in," Niema said, laughing.

"Wait, why did you call her here?"

"Hmm, yeah, Ny...what the hell is going on?" Endy asked.

"She's our ticket to getting YaYa's ass out of here, remember? Do y'all have a better idea?" asked Niema as she folded her arms.

"No," they replied in unison.

Rocko opened the door and led Keosha to the congregation.

"Come on in and sit down, Keosha. I got some info that you need to hear," said Niema.

"What do I need to know?"

"Girl, I need to tell you something about your man and my cousin. They are messing around, and we got proof," Niema blurted out.

"Are you kidding me right now? What proof do you have?"

Niema pulled up the video on her phone and said, "Here."

Keosha watched the video in silence until it came to an end.

"Oh. So, they want to play like that, huh? I can't believe these sorry motherfuckers. I'm taking Cadence and getting the fuck away from that bastard. It's about to be on like popcorn. I can't believe that asshole!" Keosha growled.

"We got a plan. This shit got to be strategic. We have the element of surprise on them since they think nobody knows," stated Endy.

"I'm definitely not letting this shit slide. I'm so tired of his cheating ass. This is the final straw," Keosha declared.

"He's going to always be who he is. Now, are you in or out?" asked Niema. "We only have one chance to do this."

AFTER THE BETRAYAL

"I'm in."

♦ ❤ ♦ RoyaltyCrowned ♦ ❤ ♦

Aunt Sally was sitting outside enjoying the weather when YaYa pulled up.

"Niyana, I know damn well you didn't just get out of that car with CJ!"

Ignoring her aunt, YaYa asked, "Where's Lil' Jay? Did Evelyn bring him yet?"

"I know your trifling ass heard me."

"It's not that deep, Auntie. He was just telling me what to do to get my baby back, that's all."

"YaYa, I don't know what you're thinking when you do the things you do. Honey, you better start thinking about that baby boy of yours before it's too late. What if Evelyn caught y'all? They already temporarily stripped him from you. Don't let it be permanent."

Aunt Sally stormed into the kitchen.

YaYa stuck out her tongue after Aunt Sally turned her back, then plopped down on the sofa and pulled out her cell phone to text Caine:

Yo, we got to do this shit fast. My aunt just flipped out because she saw you drop me off.

Caine: Chill, ma. Don't worry about nothing. Just stick to the plan, and you gon' have Lil' Jay back in no time. Trust me.

I need to get my baby back so I can get to New Orleans and say goodbye to New York forever.

There was an almost persistent knock at the door.

Yo, I got to go, but keep me posted.

"You couldn't have bothered to get the door, Niyana?!" Aunt Sally rebuked from the kitchen and then raced to open the door herself.

"Oh, hi, Endy," Aunt Sally said, her apron marked with stains of her recent feats in the kitchen. "What brings you by here?"

"Well, I was hoping YaYa was here so we could talk," replied Endy.

Aunt Sally backed away from the door so Endy could see YaYa sitting on the sofa.

"Yes. She's right here."

When YaYa jumped up in angry confusion, Endy raised her hands to show that she came in peace.

Endy took a seat across from her and said, "YaYa, look. I think it's time we talked and end this silly beef. These kids will be a part of each other's lives at some point, and I'm tired of carrying around all of this animosity towards you. All I want right now is peace in my life."

"I've apologized a million times. Everyone's mad at me, and it takes two to tango."

"You're absolutely right. This is why I want us to move past the drama and at least co-exist for the sake of the children and the rest of the family. So, are we cool?" Endy asked as she extended her hand out to YaYa.

YaYa was in shock, but she still extended her hand out.

"You're right, Endy. It would be in the best interest of the kids if we all got along. I don't want him to take my baby to spite me but because he really wants him. When he acts like a man, we will be okay."

"Well, that's where you and him have to find some common ground and communicate. I won't be the middleman for y'all, but I will put a bug in his ear to be more verbal and treat you better. I'm moving to a more peaceful space in my life, and I don't want any negative energy to exist."

"I respect that. And I know I said it before, but I truly am sorry about all this nonsense."

Endy stood up and began to make her way to the door, but before leaving, she turned around and asked, "One thing before I go. What made you sleep with Jay? I thought we were somewhat cool. Like who came on to who?"

YaYa wasn't expecting that and felt ashamed when confronted with the question.

"I don't know, honestly. It started the weekend we were all in Atlantic City. I wanted to stop, but I started developing feelings. Before I knew it, we were having sex more and more. At the time, I didn't consider the what-ifs. I certainly didn't think about the what-ifs of having a baby."

She watched as Endy's face remained neutral despite her blunt confession.

"I appreciate your honesty."

There was another knock at the door.

"Who is it?" YaYa yelled out.

Nobody responded.

When YaYa opened the door, she felt sick to her stomach.

"Hello, ladies! How y'all doing?" a cheerful Evelyn greeted as she grinned and cooed at Lil' Jay.

Endy followed up behind YaYa and walked out. "I'm going to leave so you can have some time with your son."

"Endy, don't run on my account. I'm just bringing the baby to see his mother for a little while. Glad to see you two becoming friends," retorted Evelyn as she handed YaYa the baby.

YaYa grabbed the car seat and turned around to put him on the couch. When she returned to the door, she drew back her arm and unleashed a powerful punch to Evelyn's right eye.

Evelyn stumbled back, and Endy ran to block YaYa's next punch.

"YaYa! No! Stop it!" hollered Endy as she pulled her back into the house.

Aunt Sally came running to the front of the house. She saw Evelyn holding her eye and YaYa struggling against Endy.

"YaYa! What the hell are you doing, girl?"

"Fuck that bitch! She took my baby because her son's a whore!" screamed YaYa.

Evelyn made her way to the front step, being mindful of staying out of Yaya's reach before shouting into the house, "Give me back my got damn grandson!"

"I'm so sorry, Evelyn. Please, don't do this. I got him," Aunt Sally begged, blocking the doorway.

YaYa lunged at Evelyn once again.

"Fuck her! I'm going to black that other eye!"

"YaYa, you got to calm down. This is your auntie's house, and your son is right over there watching you," whispered Endy in her ear.

The mention of her son seemed to calm YaYa down because she began looking back and forth between Evelyn and Lil' Jay. She realized she wouldn't be able to spend time with her baby boy as she planned. Endy knew this, as well. So, she tried to get YaYa to go to the kitchen.

"Why y'all have to mess with my baby? Why won't you just let me and my son be?" YaYa called out as Endy dragged her to the kitchen.

"Give me my damn grandson right now!" a black-eyed Evelyn screamed at Aunt Sally.

"Ev, you know this isn't right. Don't do this to that girl. She loves her baby."

"Hell no! I don't want my grandbaby nowhere around her psychotic ass! Y'all will be hearing from my lawyer, and I'm going for full custody now!" yelled Evelyn as she charged into the house to retrieve Lil' Jay.

"Evelyn, please let's talk about this. Please don't do this," begged Aunt Sally as she followed Evelyn to the car.

Her words fell on deaf ears. Evelyn jumped into her truck and immediately called Jay.

As Evelyn peeled away, she rolled down the window and shouted, "Tell that hoe to

AFTER THE BETRAYAL

get ready because she won't be seeing Lil' Jay ever again."

ALL THE WAY UP

Chapter 13

While in Brooklyn, Niema wanted to get some food from her favorite restaurant. As she pulled up to the restaurant that night, she spotted Caine.

"What's good, Ny?"

"What do you want? Are you following me?"

"Don't flatter yourself, sweetheart. This is my favorite spot, too. Remember?"

"Okay, well, it was nice seeing you."

Just as she tried to walk away, Caine snatched her by the arm and turned her back around.

"So, you think this shit you doing is cute or something?"

"Boy, if you don't get your hands off me. What the hell is wrong with you? Are you high or something?"

"You're a whole slut out here, Ny. Like, for real, come on...you went and had a baby with the homie."

"Look, motherfucker! If you don't get your damn hands off me, it's about to be a problem. You must be smoking if you think I owe you an explanation."

She tried to snatch herself away, but he grabbed tighter.

"Bitch, I made you. I'm the reason why that corny-ass motherfucker even looked at you."

"Caine...let me go! You're hurting my arm," whimpered Niema.

"You hurt me, bitch! And did you even give a fuck? No! You just got with the next man, opened your legs, and got pregnant!" said Caine, squeezing her arm tighter.

"Stop! You're hurting my arm! Stop it, you fucking jerk!"

Before she could utter another plea, he smacked the shit out of her, making her drop her purse and phone. She could feel her lip split and her cheek sting like hell.

A man walked up and helped Niema up before turning to Caine.

"Yo, CJ, you tripping! This a female," the man said as he shoved Caine.

After they tussled for a few minutes, another man walked up by the name of Seven. The man knew the men and broke them up.

"Ny? You alright, sweetheart?" Seven asked.

"You sorry motherfucker! My baby father gon' fuck you up again, you dopehead!" screamed Niema as she tried to get around Seven to get at Caine.

Caine looked around and ran to his car. Niema ran to her car and tried to get to her gun but was too late; Caine had already sped off.

"Calm down, ma. And put that heat away. You don't need that. He's gone," said Knowledge, the other man who had initially stepped in.

"Thank y'all so much. I don't know what would've happened if y'all didn't walk up. Oh, my God! Look at my face and my lip. Roc is gonna fucking flip," cried Niema as she looked at her reflection on her phone's cracked screen.

Niema got in her car and drove off, trying to figure out where she was gonna go. She knew she couldn't go straight home. She definitely couldn't call Endy. So, she ended up calling the only person she could go to at this point.

"What's up, Ari? Where you at? I need you to meet me, please."

"Girl, what's up? You good?"

"No, I need you to meet me downtown ASAP. CJ just hit me, and I don't want Rocko to get into any trouble on my account," Niema said in between sobs.

"Okay, let me throw on something. I will meet you at the Starbucks downtown."

"Okay. See you in a few, sis."

Before Niema could put her phone down, Rocko's name appeared on the buzzing screen.

"Oh, shit! It's Roc."

She let it go to voicemail, strapped on her seatbelt, and headed to Starbucks. She needed to figure out how she was going to face Rocko. She and Ari pulled up at the same time. Niema quickly jumped out and rushed into Ari's car.

When Niema looked up, Ari was stunned. She could not believe her eyes. Her friend sat with a bruised face and a fat lip.

"Ny, what the hell? I know Caine didn't do this shit!" Ari screamed, making a few bystanders look at the car.

"Shhh...Ari. People are looking."

"Did Caine do this to you?"

"Yes. He caught me by myself. I tried to grab something to eat, and he was out there. I don't want Rocko to know," cried Niema.

"Fuck that, Ny! We're going to Nana's, and you're going to tell him. You can't hide a swollen face and busted lip. Just tell him the truth and let the police handle it," advised Ari.

"Okay, let's go. I have to call Endy and Chynna because they're the only ones who will be able to calm him down," sighed Niema.

AFTER THE BETRAYAL

They headed to Luella's, and Niema was shitting bricks. She knew Rocko's reaction was not going to be good. He even told her not to go to that area alone, but she didn't listen.

◆ ❤ ◆ RoyaltyCrowned ◆ ❤ ◆

YaYa was heated.

"Why the fuck did you put your hands on Niema?!"

"Oh, now you worried about your cousin? I just pushed her hoe-ass down. Forget about her. Bring that phat ass over here."

Caine watched as YaYa swagged her way to him. He had been high out of his mind since Niema had a baby with Rocko.

Yaya stopped a few inches from him and gave him a disgusted look.

"I will always love my cousin. What we had ain't shit. We were drunk and high. The shit should have never happened."

"Well, it did! So, how you think your cousin gonna feel? Especially when she finds out you're fucking the love of her life." Caine joked.

"Dude, you're really sick, you know that? Ny ain't thinking about your ass! She's in love with Roc. You need to take your delusional ass on somewhere."

"You must be delusional, too! Because Jay ain't thinking about your ass either."

"Fuck you, Caine! Don't put yo' dirty-ass hands on my cousin again. Anyway, we need to figure out what we gonna do about Keosha and Jay. They're not taking my son, and you said you don't want Keosha to take Cadence," spat YaYa.

There was a knock at the door, and they both turned in surprise.

Caine jumped up, grabbed his gun from behind the couch cushion, and looked out the peephole in the door.

"Oh, shit. Where you parked at?" asked Caine in a panic.

"A couple blocks away. Why?"

"Because Jay is at the door. I forgot he was coming by. Take your ass in the room, yo!"

"What the hell?" whispered YaYa as she raced to the bedroom to hide.

The knock got louder.

"Hold up. Damn! Who is it?" Caine hollered.

He looked back to make sure YaYa was out of sight before he opened the door.

"Yo, what's up, B? Why you banging on my shit like you the police?" barked Caine when he snatched open the door.

Jasean brushed right past him and went straight to the kitchen to pour himself a shot of Hennessey.

"What's up, son? What the hell going on?" Caine asked.

"Yo, I think Endy got another dude, man!"

"What you talking about, Jay?"

"We fucked a couple of nights ago. Then she left and said some shit like thanks. That's the second time she did that bullshit," growled Jasean.

"Yo, dude, calm down. Y'all not together no more, so don't do anything stupid."

"Yo, when I find out who it is, I'm gon' lay that motherfucker down. Ain't no other dude being around my kids. She got shit fucked up, B!"

"Yo, get your phone, man. I know you hear that shit!" Caine told him as he fixed himself a shot, too.

"What's going on, ma?"

Caine's eyes immediately met Jasean's, and he knew Jasean was being told about what he did to Niema.

"Word. A'ight. We're on the way," Jasean said and hung up the phone.

AFTER THE BETRAYAL

"Why you looking at me like that?"

"Motherfucker, you know why! Why would you put your hands on Ny?! Dude, come on! You busted her lip. What the hell is wrong with you?" Jasean roared as he scooped Caine up by the collar.

"Don't tell me you care about her?" Caine laughed.

"We already got enough shit going on without you doing stupid shit."

Caine shoved Jasean back. "Fuck them! Why you mad? Is it because she's Endy's friend? Man, that broad no different than the rest of these hoes. Endy probably do have another man. Probably gonna get pregnant by him just like her hoe friend," joked Caine.

Before he could finish his sentence, Jasean thew him a right hook. They went at it for a few before YaYa decided enough was enough.

"Y'all stop! None of you bastards ain't shit!" YaYa yelled.

Jasean broke away at the sound of YaYa's voice.

"What the fuck you doing here?!"

"I'm here to tell Caine his bitch Keosha is over at Lu Lu's house every chance she gets. She ran that mouth. How the hell y'all think they know certain shit? J.J. told Lynasia she keeps them informed."

"I don't give a fuck about none of that. I asked you why the fuck are you here with my cousin!"

"Jay, it's not like that," YaYa said, her voice trembling.

Jasean crossed the room and screamed in her face, "Bitch, get the fuck out!"

"You don't have to be like that," whimpered YaYa as she inched around him to head to the door.

"Bitch, kick rocks and get the fuck out of here before it be a repeat of what just happened to your cousin!"

"Okay, Jay. I'm gone."

"You will never see my son, you fucking whore!" Jasean asked, turning his attention back to his sorry-ass cousin. "CJ, what the fuck have you done, man?"

CJ never responded. He just sat there on the floor, high out of his mind.

THIS IS HOW WE DO

Chapter 14

"**Y**o, please tell me this dude is not that stupid. Tell me he did not put his hands on my fucking girl!" Rocko roared as he sunk his fist through the wall.

The strike was so loud that he startled the ladies.

"Roc, calm down. I don't need you doing nothing crazy!" Luella screamed, grabbing his other hand and leading him to the couch.

"Ma, this motherfucker touched my girl! He's a dead man!"

Luella wanted to handle the situation the right way. Niema was scared to death because she didn't want Rocko to go to jail, get hurt, or hurt someone else. Deep down, she knew he was not going to let it go, though.

"Roc, you got your girls to think about right now. They don't need both their parents in jail," Chynna said, hoping to get through to him.

"Rocko, let the police handle it. We got to stop taking matters into our own hands. It never ends well," soothed Endy as she cradled his injured hand.

"A'ight. Let the police handle this shit, but I'm telling y'all now that punk motherfucker will see me soon!" asserted Rocko before walking off to the kitchen.

Ding, dong! Ding, dong!

"I got it. Hopefully, it's the slow-ass cops," Chynna said as she ran to answer the door. "It's Keosha. Should I let her in?"

"Yes. She got some explaining to do," replied Endy.

Keosha walked in and gave everyone a little wave, feeling the tension in the air.

"Are you behind this bullshit?" asked Endy.

"Behind what? I'm confused right now. What's going on? I only came here to give y'all some tea," said Keosha.

"Your man put his hands on Niema! The police are on the way. Look at what he did," Endy said, gesturing towards Niema.

"Oh, my!"

"Yeah, he put his hands on me. I ran into him on Fulton when I was about to get something to eat. He was in his feelings about me having a baby with Roc. He slapped me and busted my lip," explained Niema.

"Oh, my God... I swear to y'all I didn't know he did that or was going to do that. I need to get Cadence away from all of them. Well, we need to talk because shit got deeper between YaYa and Caine," revealed Keosha.

"What's up?" asked Chynna.

"I know something went down between CJ and YaYa. I saw it firsthand today."

"Are you sure, Keosha?" Niema asked.

"I wouldn't play about that shit. I got home, and the door wasn't shut all the way. I heard CJ and Jay arguing. Next thing, I heard a female voice. After that, I heard Jay yelling and telling YaYa to get out. He told her that she wasn't going to see Lil' Jay again. I also heard him say if she didn't leave, it was gon' be a repeat of what happened to her cousin," Keosha shared.

AFTER THE BETRAYAL

"This chick is being an all-out thot. Even after we tried to make amends with her, she is still doing trifling bullshit. I hate that I even fell for it," huffed Endy.

"Me too," said Niema.

"I'ma tell your ass this once. If you don't leave that bastard, you're crazy. He's careless and disrespectful," stated Endy.

"Endy, I'm out...believe me when I say it. YaYa and Lynasia already know I've been talking to y'all. I got to get Cadence away from that crazy motherfucker before it's too late. Now, I have a way we can get them all out the way, but y'all got to be ready. Endy, you know what we have to do," said Keosha.

"Yeah, I do, and we're all in. Let's finish this," Endy replied.

◆ ❤ ◆ RoyaltyCrowned ◆ ❤ ◆

"Yo, son, you dead wrong. You know this shit about to escalate like hell. Roc's not gonna let that shit go," groaned Jasean as he ran his hands down his face.

"Motherfucker, that was my woman for ten years! You think I was gonna let her go? Fuck them! If they want me, then I'm ready for war!"

Jasean ignored him.

Evelyn and Marilyn came rushing through the door.

"CJ, this is your mother talking to you! If Keosha leaves with Cadence, we may not see her ever again. You need to find a way to fix this shit. Stop stuffing that white devil up your damn nose and start thinking before you react. Niema don't owe you shit. You cheated on her and had a baby. Another thing, what's this bullshit I heard about YaYa hiding in your bedroom?" berated Marilyn.

"Ma, it ain't even like that. YaYa tried to help me figure out what fuck shit KiKi has been on. She been real close to Endy and Ny lately. I wanted to know what they trying to stir up. I got mad as hell when I saw Ny, and my emotions took over. I fucked up, Ma. Niema was a good woman to me. I thought I had time to get my shit together," mumbled Caine.

"Well, baby, that's the way of the universe. Those girls gave y'all every opportunity to get your shit together, but y'all both continued to play the streets. So, now both of you have to suffer the consequences. Endy and Niema don't owe y'all shit," Evelyn added.

"I got it! I was high as hell. Ny knows I didn't mean no harm. I'm just still mad about the whole Roc situation. So, I guess I got to see this dude for now," said Caine.

"Boy, do you hear yourself?! That girl asked your ol' nasty ass to stop fucking with them little hoes. You continued to do you, and you broke her down until she couldn't take no more. Stop with the bullshit and suck it up like a real man," replied Marilyn.

"Yo, who side you on?"

"I'm on the side that's right, and that damn sure ain't yours."

Marilyn stormed out of the living room, and Evelyn ran behind her to calm her down.

Ding, dong!

Jasean got up and looked through the peephole.

"Oh, shit. It's the fucking police," whispered Jasean.

"What?! Why they here?" whispered Caine as he jumped up to head to the back of the house.

Evelyn returned to the front room, and Jasean told her who was at the door.

"I got it. Get out the way. Who is it?" Evelyn asked from behind the door.

"NYPD. Ma'am, can you open the door?"

Jasean raced to the sofa and sat down.

"Ma, open the door."

Evelyn opened up the door and was greeted by two officers.

"Hello, ma'am. We're here to talk to Caine Newman. We have a complaint of assault against Niema Mason," said the officer.

"Marilyn, the police are here!" Evelyn yelled down the hall.

"What is it?" questioned Marilyn as she came to the door.

"The cops are here. It's about the situation with Ny," Evelyn whispered to her.

Looking at the officers, Marilyn recognized one of them. His name was Clay; he was one of the officers who raided Endy and Jasean's house when he got locked up for the extortion charges the year before. Clay wasn't fond of the Newman family, so it would bring him some joy to lock up Caine.

"It wasn't assault! We got to arguing, and she jumped in my face. I pushed her back! It was self-defense," shouted Caine from the back of the house.

"Well, that's not what Ms. Mason and witnesses told us. Plus, she has a bruise on her face and a busted lip. We need you to come to the station because she wants to press charges against you," Officer Clay yelled back.

"Man, you don't have no proof of shit. I'm not going nowhere with y'all," said Caine as he walked to the sofa.

"CJ, please don't make a scene. Just go with the police. We're right behind you," begged Marilyn.

"Ma, fuck no! I didn't do shit. These pigs gonna have to drag me off this couch and out of here."

"Sir, we are going to ask you one more time to put your hands behind your back and come with us!" yelled Officer Clay, drawing his taser.

"CJ, please cut the bullshit. Just go on. We coming right behind you. Your baby girl is right there in the other room. Don't be stupid," said Evelyn.

"Fuck these pigs! I'm not about to go——"

Before he could finish his sentence, the officers tackled him on the couch and slammed him down on the floor. Jasean went and grabbed Cadence and slipped to the back of the house so she wouldn't see her dad fighting the police. Marilyn jumped on Officer Clay to help Caine.

"Marilyn, stop!" Evelyn shouted while trying to pull her sister off the cop. "You're going to go to jail!"

Marilyn didn't care; she continued to pound Clay until he managed to restrain him. He then called for back-up while his partner finished restraining Caine.

"Fuck y'all! This shit's not legal! How y'all gonna go by her word?!" shouted Caine as he struggled in his handcuffs.

After about ten minutes, four more police officers arrived. Caine and Marilyn were arrested. Evelyn was livid because now she had to go to the precinct and bail both of them out. Once the police left, she called Keosha to meet her so she could get the baby.

"KiKi, I need you to meet me to get Cadence ASAP. I have to bail Marilyn and CJ out of jail," Evelyn told her.

"Okay, sure. Where you want me to meet you?"

"Meet me on Ralph Avenue and Chauncy Street."

Evelyn yelled for Jay to grab Cadence. Once everyone was out the door, they locked Caine's door and headed to the car.

♦ ❤ ♦ RoyaltyCrowned ♦ ❤ ♦

"I have to go get Cadence. The police just arrested Caine and Marilyn," said Keosha after getting off the phone.

"We're not in the clear yet. I need you to go ahead and meet her. We are going to head to the precinct to file these charges and a restraining order. Then I'm gonna see who this chick is that you said Jay got sniffing around my store. You do know it's no turning back now, right?" Endy said.

"I'm ready to get my daughter the fuck away from that crazy-ass family. I'm gon' lay low while the plan pans out. Also, that chick is a Hispanic that used to date this big-time dealer. She's been cozy with him and knew every time you left to go to North Carolina and shit."

"Let's get to the station. Aye, Keosha, you know if you need us, hit up Endy's phone or mine. Just don't hit Ny's because you know they gon' be asking her hella questions," Rocko said as Keosha made her way toward the door.

"Thanks, y'all. We got to find out who the chick is helping him. Is she some private investingator or something?" asked Keosha.

"Oh, believe me, I'm going to know something soon," Endy assured her.

They all left the house at once to go handle business.

LOYAL

Chapter 15

Ring, ring, ring!

"Hi, may I speak to Endyia, please?" said a strange voice on Luella house phone.

"May I ask who's calling? And why you didn't call her on her cell?"

"I'm sorry. This is her realtor from North Carolina. My name is Sincere Richmond. I've been trying to reach her on her cell all day, but there was no answer. She told me in case of emergencies or anything important about her properties to call this number, ma'am," the male voice responded.

"Well, Mr. Richmond, she's not here. I will tell her you called," Luella said bluntly and hung up.

"Nana, what you down there mumbling about?" Karishma asked her.

"Do you know anything about this Mr. Richmond and Endy having some properties in North Carolina?" Luella asked.

"What's up, fam bam?" Endy greeted them as she came through the door with her kids in tow.

Karishma was saved by Endy walking in.

"Speaking of the damn devil! We need to talk," Luella spat with her hands on her hips.

"What's up, Nana? What you talking about?" Endy screwed up her face, confused.

"Who the hell is this Mr. Richmond? Why did he say he needed to talk to you about your properties?"

"It's not that serious, Nana. He's a man who helped me find a couple of commercial properties in Carolina. I am expanding the boutique, that's all. Wait, why did he call here? Let me call him right quick to see what he wanted. I'll be right back!"

Endy frantically rushed to the kitchen to return his call.

"Hello, everyone!" Tanya shouted as she walked in with her sisters Lisa and Keisha.

"Okay, Pablo! He did that with the coat and boots, Mommy. I know he brought you that," Keisha complimented her mother.

"You know he keep me fly but umm, where are the girls? I thought we were all doing this together?" Luella questioned.

"Mommy, they're meeting us at the mall," Lisa answered, ready to go.

"Well, family, I hate to be the bearer of bad news, but I have to shoot to Carolina really quick," Endy said hurriedly, grabbing her things.

"What? When are you leaving?" Luella asked with a disappointed look.

"Immediately, Nana. I have to tie up some loose ends business-wise if I want the store to be open on New Year's."

By the look on their faces, they all appeared to be frustrated. Luella immediately walked out. Endy was hurt to bail on her family, but there was nothing she could do at that point. She had put too much hard work and time into her North Carolina location.

"Well, baby, you're grown. Mommy will be okay. Go get your coins in order," Lisa told her niece and gave her a high-five.

"Thanks, Auntie! I promise y'all once everyone gets down South, y'all are going to be so proud of me. I have to make sure my kids and me are straight after this divorce," Endy told them.

She hugged everyone as they left out the door.

"Okay, baby. I want you to be sure that you're careful, that's all," Tanya explained.

"Yes, Ma. I'm good. I promise."

♦ ♥ ♦ Royalty Crowned ♦ ♥ ♦

"Niyana, are you ready? We have to leave soon. You don't want to be late to court!" Aunt Sally yelled up the stairs.

"I'm coming!" YaYa yelled back.

YaYa stared at her reflection in the mirror, praying she would be able to bring her baby boy home. She donned a navy-blue DK suit with a beige ruffled blouse, and navy/beige plaid pumps and her hair hanging in big, beautiful curls. She was dressed to the tee. She looked like a woman about her business. This was the YaYa everyone was used to.

"Niyana Bradley, if you don't bring your ass on here!"

"Okay, I'm coming."

"I told you I don't want to be late. It's not a good look."

"Auntie, I got you! We good."

"Girl, bring your ass on."

They quickly got in the car and headed to the family court building. YaYa was nervous as hell. She knew Jasean wasn't ready to be a full-time dad, and as much as Evelyn loved her grandson, she did not want to be tied down with no child. YaYa was ready to get this court mess over with. They made it with fifteen minutes to spare, and YaYa could feel the dirty looks from Evelyn.

"Please, stand. The Honorable Judge William Watkins is presiding!" shouted the bailiff.

God, please let this go in my favor, YaYa prayed as everyone stood up.

"We are here today to discuss the future custody of baby Jasean Mason Newman, Jr.," announced Judge Watkins as the gavel slammed down, signaling everyone in the courtroom to take a seat.

The doors to the courtroom opened, and in walked Niema and Keosha. They both walked on the side of the Newman family. Funny how things came back around—YaYa did the same thing to Rocko when he went to court with Taiya. It was only right that Niema returned the favor.

"I know this bitch did not come to court on their behalf, Auntie," YaYa groaned.

"Keep calm, baby girl. I will handle Ny," said Aunt Sally as she glared at Niema.

"I would like to call Niema Mason to the stand, Your Honor," said Jasean's attorney, Robert Currin.

"You're a disloyal bitch!" screamed YaYa.

"Niema, what are you doing?" cried Aunt Sally.

"Order in the court! Order, I said!" yelled Judge Watkins as he slammed his gavel.

"Please, quiet down before y'all ruin everything. Let me handle this," replied Jimmy Ratcliffe, YaYa's lawyer.

"I apologize, Your Honor," Aunt Sally said.

"Yeah, I apologize," said YaYa.

Niema was sworn under oath.

"Ms. Mason, how well do you know Ms. Bradley?" asked Currin.

"She's my first cousin," responded Niema.

"Can you tell me how you know Mr. Newman?"

"He was married to my best friend until he had an affair with YaYa."

"So, the baby is a byproduct of their affair?"

"Yes."

"Do you have any concerns for Ms. Bradley as a mother?"

"Yes, she has gotten very vindictive, mean, and suicidal. I'm worried the baby may not be safe," Niema stated.

"You know what, Ny? Fuck you! Fuck all of y'all," roared YaYa as she stood up.

"Order in the court!" Judge Watkins yelled.

"She's lying. You're just mad because you think I fucked Caine. You have no loyalty to your family!" cried YaYa as she kicked off her heels to get to Niema.

"Get her out of here!" yelled the judge to the guards.

"Niyana, please calm down, baby!" pleaded Aunt Sally as the guards rushed toward YaYa.

"Fuck all y'all! Fuck this court! Fuck the judge, the lawyers, Jay, and his family! Fuck all y'all!" yelled YaYa as the bailiff cuffed her.

She cursed and screamed all the way to the holding cells.

"Niema, how can you do this to your own blood?" sobbed Aunt Sally.

"It had to be done," Niema coolly stated.

"I said order in the court! Sit down, ma'am!" Judge Watkins said firmly.

Aunt Sally sat down defeatedly and cried into her hands while Evelyn sat back with a devilish grin on her face. The judge looked flustered and upset. YaYa already blew it, and Aunt Sally knew it.

"This court is adjourned. We will convene tomorrow morning at nine o'clock. Until then, the baby will remain in the paternal grandmother's care," said Judge Watkins as he hit his gavel on the stand, finalizing the session.

AFTER THE BETRAYAL

The following day, everyone was in court on time. The court released YaYa on her own recognizance. The hearing proceeded without any hiccups, and now it was time for deliberation.

"Please rise!" the bailiff shouted.

Everyone stood for the judge to enter the courtroom.

"Make sure you keep your mouth closed, Niyana," mumbled Aunt Sally.

"After hearing everyone's statements and arguments, the final decision concerning Jasean Mason Newman Jr. is the child will remain in the custody of his paternal grand-mother with--"

"What! How the hell did she get custody? Her son is a fucking drug dealer! It's the holidays! You really going to do this, Ev?!" roared YaYa, interrupting the judge.

"Ma'am, you have really tried my patience. Now I will send you back to the holding cell again, but this time, I will make sure you sit for forty-eight hours!" warned Judge Watkins.

"My apologies, Judge. I love my baby," wept YaYa.

"Now, if I can continue, the baby will remain with his paternal grandmother, with the mother having visitation twice a week and every other weekend. Ms. Bradley will need to complete a mental health assessment as well as parenting and anger management classes before the next court date to see if she is eligible for increased visitation rights. Next court date is set six months from today. Court is adjourned."

PROMISE

Chapter 16

That next week, the entire family flew down to Raleigh, North Carolina. Luella, Pablo, Tanya, Eddie, Marlo, and Lisa stayed with Aunt Linda. Chynna, Reeko, Ari, and Tylon stayed at Niema and Rocko's house. The rest of Endy's family got hotel rooms. All her family met up at her aunt Linda's house so they could arrive downtown together.

"Well, what time are we supposed to be there?" asked Luella.

"Endy said the cars are supposed to be here in a few. Just make sure y'all ready."

Two stretched Hummer limos pulled up at the house, and everyone climbed in. They were excited to see what Endy had done with the new store. About thirty minutes later, they arrived downtown in front of Endy's new store.

"Oh, my! Now, this is gorgeous!" gasped Tanya as she stepped out of the limo.

The new E-Class was decorated with an arch of purple, white, and black balloons and a black carpet rolled out. Everyone was dressed to kill. When they all got out of their limos, they lined up for a group photo. Endy had photographers, the news station, and a lot of business people in attendance. Everyone's attention was drawn to her as she stepped on a stage to speak.

"I want to thank everyone for coming out, especially my family who came all the way from New York. I want everyone to enjoy themselves. So please, eat, drink, shop, and mingle!" Endy announced.

Everyone started clapping enthusiastically as she exited the stage and took the giant scissors to cut the ribbon in front of the store. Endy was proud of herself, and she could tell her family was, too. Everyone danced and mingled during the celebration except one man—Mr. Sincere Richmond. He stood at the bar sipping his drink while his eyes remained glued to Endy.

"Chynna, who is that tall cup of sexiness over there?" asked Asia.

"That's Rich, Endy's realtor. Ain't he fine, girl?"

"Yeah, and guess what? He's clocking Endy's every move," Asia said, tracing the movement of his eyes.

Endy wore a purple open-back mermaid-styled satin dress that showed all her curves. Rich couldn't keep his eyes off her. He wanted her in the worst way, but he knew he had to keep it professional with all the family watching him. After three hours passed, Endy let the family know she had one more surprise for them.

"Do you know what this surprise is, Chynna?" Lisa asked her daughter.

"Nah. She just told me that we are going to love it."

The family piled up in the limos to head to the surprise. Endy was nervous as shit, but there was no turning back. Once they were there, she asked everyone to get out of the vehicles. The house they stopped at was gorgeous. Some of the family figured it was a place she rented to have the New Year's party.

"Well, family...this is my surprise. I bought a house here. Me and the kids are moving to North Carolina," Endy screamed enthusiastically.

Her family rushed forward to hug and kiss her. They were ecstatic. However, Luella and Tanya weren't too thrilled about the idea—especially now that they had to tell her Jasean was about to take her to court for the kids.

"We will talk to her tomorrow. I can't ruin my baby's moment," mumbled Tanya.

"Baby, this house is gorgeous. I know you're going to kill the décor for real once you get all moved in," Egypt commented while giving Endy another big hug.

"Get y'all a glass of champagne. It's countdown time," slurred Keisha as the new year began to approach.

"Here we go, y'all!" Rocko yelled as he grabbed Niema's hand.

The family had the broadcast from Times Square on the big projector screen. Everyone began the countdown.

"10, 9, 8, 7, 6, 5, 4, 3, 2, 1...Happy New Year!"

"Hmm, do you see that?" gasped Luella as she nudged Tanya.

"See what?" said Tanya, quickly turning around.

Endy and Rich were kissing. At this point, all the family had turned around, waiting for the happy couple to explain.

"Oh well, the cat is out of the bag. Rich and I are a couple; we've been a couple for a while. This explains my frequent trips," stated Endy boldly.

"Wait, is this Rich from all those years ago?" interrupted Chynna.

"Yes. This is Sincere Richmond, the one I dated years ago. We reconnected, and I love him," Endy confessed.

"Well, congratulations!" blurted out Lisa.

"Live your life, cuz! Congratulations," Chynna said warmly, going in for another hug.

Lord, let me enjoy this night, because tomorrow is going to be a mess, Tanya thought as she downed her drink.

LOVE KNOCKS YOU DOWN

Chapter 17

Jasean was finally having his day in court. His lawyer, Matthew Currin, and his family were with him. Currin was one of the best defense attorneys in New York. As Jasean waited for court to start, the doors opened, and two FBI agents walked in. Both Evelyn and Jasean looked at each other in confusion. Jasean instantly became nervous and agitated. The agents walked over and whispered to Lydia Garrett, the prosecutor.

"Currin, what the fuck is this?" asked Jasean as he leaned over.

"Jay, please chill out. Don't panic, son," whispered Evelyn.

"I don't know, Mr. Newman, but I'm sure we're about to find out," responded Currin.

"All rise! The Honorable Judge Knowles presiding," yelled the bailiff.

"Does the prosecution have their first witness?" asked Judge Knowles.

"Your Honor, the prosecution rests, as the federal government has picked up the case. The defendant will be placed in federal custody effective immediately for two accounts of first-degree murder. There's a federal witness who is willing to testify. They have been placed in witness protection while the FBI proceeds with their investigation," explained Lydia Garrett.

"Ma'am, I'm Agent Baker, and this is Agent Jones. We have a search warrant for your premises as well as one for Mr. Jasean Newman's resident," stated Agent Baker.

"What? I ain't going nowhere with y'all," spat Jasean.

"Wait! Jay, be quiet. So, you're arresting him for what? For hearsay?" Evelyn shouted.

"Ma'am, I need you to stand back! Mr. Newman, you're under arrest for the murders of Serious Jones and Duron 'Chubb' Wright," replied Agent Baker, grabbing his handcuffs from his waist.

Jasean swung sideways when Agent Baker attempted to handcuff him, which prompted the officers to tackle him to the floor.

"Jay, don't resist, baby! Can someone please tell me what's going on?" Evelyn pleaded helplessly. "I'm not understanding any of this. Please, tell me what's going on!"

"Ma'am, you need to go home, and someone will be in touch with you," Agent Jones ordered.

After Evelyn calmed down, they informed her that agents had already been sent to her house to search the premises. She called Marilyn and Juan, Reeko's uncle, to meet her there.

♦ ❤ ♦ RoyaltyCrowned ♦ ❤ ♦

"Thanks, Nina, for coming on such short notice," Endy said.

"Girl, I got your back. I can't believe Jay is now facing murder charges. Do you know who this witness is?" asked Nina.

"Girl, no! It's crazy, but sometimes your demons catch up with you. Jay had a lot going on in the streets, but at least he kept all that away from home. I'm ready to close out my business here and move my ass down South with my new man."

"Hmm, new man, huh?" Nina teased.

"Yes, girl! He's a blast from the past. I used to date him some years ago when me and Jay broke up. His name is Rich; he's from Harlem. He used to play the streets, but now he's a very successful realtor. He's the one who helped me with the store and new house down South."

Endy glowed as she explained her whirlwind love.

"Rich from Harlem! Okay, I see why you're in such a great mood!" Nina giggled.

"Nina, it's so different than what I'm used to with Jay. I love that he's legit and all about me."

"Endy, I need you to be careful, though. You're a beautiful and successful woman. I would hate to see another man have you caught up in some mess."

"Girl, Jay is the only mess I had in my life. Now that the divorce is final, I can move on with my life and be happy. Rich wants to get married and have children of his own. He doesn't have any yet, which is a plus. That means no baby mama drama, you feel me," laughed Endy.

"Well, as long as you're happy, I'm for it. I just know a lot of these men seem great in the beginning and then turn out to be nightmares."

"Girl, stop. You will find your Prince Charming someday."

"I get it, girl. I'm all for real love. We need more of it in this crazy world," Nina responded as she grabbed her bag.

"Nina, thank you for everything you've done. I will see you in a few weeks to finalize the lease for the midtown store. I'm ready to turn it over to Rizzy. I think she's ready to take over now."

"Okay. You enjoy your trip to P.R. and don't do anything I wouldn't do," laughed Nina while walking to the door.

"Hell, I'm going to do it all and more."

"You're so nasty, girl. I'll speak to you soon," Nina said as she hugged Endy.

"Okay, boo. Talk to you later," Endy replied as she walked her out.

♦ ♥ ♦ RoyaltyCrowned ♦ ♥ ♦

"Girl, would you take your tail on and get ready for your trip? It's almost one o'clock," yelled Tanya.

"I know, Ma. I just want to make sure everything is in place before I leave my babies," Endy replied as she kissed her kids on the forehead.

They both sat eating in their highchairs, enjoying their food. Patience was now eighteen months and Peace was seven months. She had to meet Niema downtown Brooklyn so they could shop before their trip to Puerto Rico.

"Okay, Mommy! I'm about to head out. Call me if you need me," Endy said, grabbing her purse.

"You look so happy. You deserve to be happy, baby. Remember, leave your past completely behind you. If you gonna go, then go all the way," advised Tanya as she kissed Endy on the cheek.

"Thanks, Mommy. Believe me, I am. I'll be back after a while."

Endy jumped in her car and put her earpiece in to call Chynna and Niema to let them know she was on the way.

"Hey, girls. I'm like ten minutes away. I will see y'all in a few," Endy told them as she sped down the parkway.

"Okay, girl. We just got here, so don't rush. See you soon," replied Chynna, hanging up.

AFTER THE BETRAYAL

"I know that's not Endy's ass being late again," Niema commented, laughing.

"Yup, even though she's the main one who's always telling us not to be late." Chynna cracked up.

"I know that's not YaYa," Niema said as she squinted her eyes, concentrating on a distant figure.

"Probably so, girl, but we're not about to let nobody ruin what is about to be an awesome V-Day weekend for us," snarled Chynna.

"Come on, let's meet Endy by Macy's on Fulton Street. You would think a near-death experience would wake her ass up," Niema snapped.

"You're right. Let's go before I smack your cousin. Some people just don't learn, girl. I'm not in the mood for her nonsense today."

As they walked up the street, Chynna's phone rang.

"Girl, where you at?" yelled Chynna at Endy.

"I'm parking right now."

"We walked up the street because we just saw YaYa's ass, girl. She even smirked and tried to be funny."

"Damn, this chick is like a gnat that won't go away." Endy laughed as she thought about YaYa's constant need for attention.

Endy met up with the girls five minutes later, and they headed into Macy's.

"Damn, bitch! Where were you coming from?" questioned Niema.

"My house," Endy shot back, then while looking around, she asked, "Where that thot go?"

"We don't know. She disappeared somewhere, girl," replied Chynna.

As they were shopping, Endy got an eerie feeling that someone was watching her. However, she ignored it and continued to shop.

"Girl, we have to get to the spa! Come on and pick out something, please. You the only chick I know who takes two hours in one damn store," Niema joked.

"I have to make sure I look good for my boo thang, girl. I feel like a schoolgirl with a crush," blushed Endy.

She had found her light again. Everything Jasean took for granted, Rich appreciates; he showed her that he did. Although he was heartbroken when she left him the first time to go back to Jasean, he always knew their love story wasn't done. He was just as in love with her as she was with him.

"Okay, hoes. Let's go, so I can get these feet done. Call Leigh and tell her we'll be there in five minutes," Endy ordered.

They were all enjoying the massages, pedicures, manicures, and facials. Rich treated them to everything. Endy hit the jackpot—and the legal jackpot at that.

As they are getting their feet done Leigh blurts out and said "One ju friends come taaday and see you come taaday," Leigh tried to explain to Endy with her broken English.

"What friend? Ari?"

"Noooo, me know Ari. Umm, don't know. She says her ju friend. Me not see hah beefor," replied Leigh.

"I don't know. Maybe it was one of my cousins. They are the only ones who knew I was coming here today. I don't know, Leigh, but this foot massage feels great," Endy commented.

"So, um, ju and Mr. Jay no together?" asked Leigh.

"No, he cheated with a thot, so I left him. My new man paid for this," responded Endy.

"I'm starving. Where we going to eat?" Chynna interrupted.

"I want some soul food. I'm tired of seafood," Niema complained.

As the ladies left the spa three hours later, they ran into Keosha and Lynasia.

"Well, hello, ladies. Glad to see y'all made up. Where y'all headed?" Chynna questioned.

AFTER THE BETRAYAL

"We're about to grab some drinks and food at Southern Soul," responded Keosha.

"Oh, that sounds good," replied Chynna as she rubbed her belly.

"Can you stop being hungry for a second?" laughed Niema.

"Hello, Lynasia. Hope all is well," Endy said.

"Hey, Endy, I'm good," Lynasia said kindly. "Me and James talked. And I would like for us to have a better relationship. Y'all know I was just trying to be loyal to my friends. I didn't know Taiya would go that far."

"Well, you were a good friend to her and Keosha, but sometimes people outgrow people," Chynna said and shrugged.

When Taiya shot Rocko, she ran to Lynasia, who was completely unaware at the time. Taiya used her house phone, and the police tracked it, making Lynasia livid because she knew everyone would think she was involved. The whole situation almost cost her family. James was upset; he took Lil' James and left the house for a few months. Her life as she knew it fell apart because of her so-called friend Taiya.

"Hmm, can we go eat now? Because a bitch is hungry," whined Chynna.

"Girl, feed your cousin," Niema chuckled.

"Come on, y'all. Let's get some food. I need a patron margarita! ASAP!"

For the first time, all the ladies were on one accord and chilling together in one room. Endy knew her nana would be proud because all she wanted was for the family to remain close. The girls were drinking, laughing, and acting silly—just enjoying each other's company.

Niema was genuinely over the situation with Keosha, and Lynasia and Keosha made up and decided to cut off YaYa. These women all had something in common: the need for peace in their lives.

After a couple of hours, the ladies prepared to go home.

"Ladies, I really enjoyed this! We must all do it again. Keosha and Lynasia, y'all, too!"

Chynna cheered.

"Yeah, this was nice. I'm glad to be finally done with that damn family. Girl, they had a bitched stressed out," replied Keosha as she raised her arms in worship.

"I know, girl. Me too! I needed peace, and the last few weeks have been good to yah girl--really good," Endy teased.

Niema laughed. "You so crazy."

After a couple of hours or good conversation, food and drinks they ladies prepared to leave. Once outside, everyone said their goodbyes and parted ways. Chynna and Lyna-sia went one way; Niema, Endy, and Keosha went the other. It was pretty cold, considering it was in the middle of winter in New York. As they got closer to the car, Endy stopped and looked around.

"Y'all heard that?" asked Endy.

"Girl, what you talking about?" Niema replied.

"I heard it, too. It was like a clicking sound," stated Keosha.

YaYa came around the corner, pointing a 9mm Luger at them. Once she saw she had them cornered, she smirked.

"Y'all some real bum-ass bitches! Now it's my time to talk, and y'all bitches gonna listen!" yelled YaYa.

"What the fuck?!" Keosha shouted.

YaYa aimed the gun at Keosha.

"You know, you one disloyal-ass bitch, KiKi. Your name is not Keosha. It's KiKi. That's your name, no matter how much you think you changed your life. Once a stripper hoe, always a stripper hoe!" YaYa spat.

"Fuck you, YaYa! You're upset with everybody because Jay don't want your ass. What good did you think was going to come from what y'all did?" yelled Keosha.

"Spare me the bullshit. I'm no different than your hoe ass," YaYa shot back.

AFTER THE BETRAYAL

"YaYa, I don't know what the fuck you on, but you tripping," interjected Endy.

YaYa tilted her head and then swung the gun in Endy's direction.

"Bitch, you need to shut your stupid ass up. You always try to act like your shit don't stink. I know you got something to do with my baby father getting locked up!" YaYa roared.

"YaYa, please don't do this. You will go to jail. You have a baby to think about, cuz," pleaded Niema.

YaYa began to laugh hysterically; she swung the gun back and forth until she stopped it on Niema.

"Oh, it's 'cuz' now! You've been running around with these bitches like I don't exist. Even the bitch who stole your man gets time with you. Now that I got this gun pointed at you, you wanna sing a different tune? Bitch, you're pathetic!" chuckled YaYa.

"YaYa, this is not cool. Like, come on... I don't give a fuck about that man. I moved on. You can have his sorry ass," Endy told her.

"Fuck all y'all. This isn't about Jay. It's about how y'all tried to defame my character and make me feel small. Y'all act like y'all perfect, but you're not," screamed YaYa.

She cocked the gun and began swinging it back and forth between her targets.

"I wonder who's gonna get hit first if I pull this trigger."

The women huddled together and whimpered.

"Aye, what's going on here?" a man shouted out his car's window as he turned down the street.

YaYa sprinted off in the dark as the man flashed his high beams their way.

"Sir, thank you. You came just in time," cried Keosha as she ran to hug the man.

Niema put her phone away and said, "The police are on the way."

"I can't believe this chick pulled a gun on us," Endy cried enraged.

"Ladies, this is Juwan our life saver. He just moved here from Panama," Keosha said, approaching the ladies with him by her side.

"I'm glad I could help. Is everyone okay?" asked Juwan.

"Yeah, thanks to you. I could have never seen my babies again," said Endy as she hugged him.

"Keosha gave me a shortened version of what happened. I'm sorry y'all went through that. I wish I would have thought to run after her," Juwan replied.

"Don't worry about that. We are forever grateful to you," stated Endy.

The police finally arrived, and the girls recounted what happened to them and what direction she fled.

"I just got off the phone with Aunt Sally and told her what YaYa did. She flipped the hell out," Niema informed them.

"Ny, baby! Where you at?" yelled Rocko as he busted through the group of onlookers.

"Baby, I'm right here! I'm okay," shouted Niema as she rushed to hug him.

"What the hell is going on with YaYa? Why the fuck would she pull a gun on y'all...and in the middle of a busy-ass neighborhood?!"

"I don't know, Roc. You should have seen the look in her eyes. I thought we were gone. That bitch cornered us and everything. She was definitely high off something," explained Endy.

"What the police say?" asked Rocko, tightening his arms around Niema.

"We told them where they could probably find her," Endy replied.

"This shit got me pissed the fuck off. She won't get away with this shit," growled Rocko.

"Roc, we're going to let the cops handle it," said Endy, perceiving the rage in his eyes.

"Someone better get through to her and fast because now she is known as armed and dangerous," Juwan informed them.

"I know I feel so sorry for her son because he's about to be without both of his par-

AFTER THE BETRAYAL

ents," Endy shook her head.

ON BENDED KNEE

Chapter 18

R ich did what all the dope boys dreamed of doing—he turned his illegal money into a legit business. He took his drug money and built a real estate empire. He sold houses worldwide with the help of some of the most prominent investors around the country. Rich gained the respect of many public officials and was sitting on a billion-dollar gold mine.

He planned to spoil Endy like he should have done years ago, but he wanted to make sure he could trust her first. He needed her to be all his—and completely over Jasean. Rich knew now was the time for him to open up to her completely.

"Mr. Richmond, all the rooms are prepared and ready for your guests," a maid told him.

"Thanks, Elsa! Can you go ahead and make sure the brunch is about ready? They should be arriving shortly."

About an hour later, Rich heard a horn outside. He rushed to the front of the villa, excited to see his baby. He hadn't seen her in a few days and missed her terribly.

"Elsa, Glenda, they're here. Please make sure the cocktails are ready," shouted Rich as he headed to greet Endy and her family.

As Endy walked toward the beautiful home with her crew, she was in awe of how big and beautiful the house was.

"Girl, this is dope, yo," whispered Niema.

The guys didn't want to seem too impressed, so they kept their facial expressions neutral.

"This is a nice-ass house! Damn, bitch, you hit the jackpot!" whispered Ari as she playfully slapped Endy on the ass.

"Girl, it's not even like that. We just fit together really well and fell in love, that's all."

When they reached the door, they were greeted by Rich's staff.

Endy spotted Rich and ran straight to him. She wasn't thinking about food or drinks; she just wanted her man.

"Baby! Oh my God! I didn't know you were going to do all this. I love it so much. Thank you!" Endy said while smothering him in kisses.

"Rich, this is really nice. I'm ready for a bae-cay!" shouted Chynna.

"What's up, fellas? Welcome to my home," Rich said as he extended his hand to each of the gentlemen.

"Oh, so this your crib crib or your crib for the week?" joked Reeko.

"This is my home. 'Deed in my name' house," replied Rich sarcastically.

Rich could tell Reeko was hazing him, but he had to let him know he was king around here. He wasn't letting anyone mess up his romantic weekend with his woman.

"This some real money moves right here," yapped Ari.

Rich just smiled and gestured them further inside the house.

"Y'all come in and get settled in your rooms."

"Sure. Let's get these bags to the room," said Reeko.

"Oh, I have staff for that. They will take your bags to your rooms while you all look around. Juan, Felix! I need y'all to take their bags upstairs."

"Aye, I can take my own shit upstairs. I don't know them!" barked Reeko, snatching his suitcases back from the staff.

Reeko was the only one acting this way because he was trying to be loyal to Jasean. He knew Jasean was wrong for how he treated Endy, but he still had to stand beside him.

"Yo, you need to chill!" snapped Endy.

"Come on, baby! I can't wait to see what the rooms look like," Niema cheered, trying to lighten the mood.

Chynna pulled Reeko to the side and laid into him. "Reek, what the fuck is up with you?"

"What? Dude trying to show off, and I'm not feeling it."

"I told you don't bring this shit on the trip. I'm here to have a good time. I know you're trying to be loyal to Jay but just stop. Hell, I'm not all that comfortable either, but we're here. So, let's enjoy it especially since we didn't have to pay for shit. We need this trip, Reek. Don't act like an ass," Chynna scolded him.

"Okay, baby. You're right. Ugh. I'm going to do better. Endy deserves this, and so do you, baby," Reeko softened, pouting as he looked at Chynna.

"Thank you. You promise to be on your best behavior?"

"I got you, ma. I promise. I'm just mad at Jay for doing this bullshit, man. This should be all of us--the original crew!"

"Well, sometimes things don't turn out the way we want them to. Let's make the best of it. Now, let's go check out our room."

While they searched for their room, Rich and Endy were compensating for lost intimacy.

Rich kissed her forehead and said, "Yo, I don't know what's dude's problem, but you know I'm not going to tolerate disrespect in my house."

AFTER THE BETRAYAL

"I'm not gonna let no one ruin this nice vacation you planned for us," hummed Endy as Rich's hand rubbed her back.

"I just want you to know I'm all-in, baby. I love you so much."

"I love you, too. I'm looking forward to starting my new life with you. I'm drained from this New York drama. I'm ready to become a southern belle," Endy teased.

"I promise to love you like you are supposed to be loved. Your children will become my children. I got y'all forever, babe. I don't think I ever stopped loving you."

"I know, baby. I can tell by how you talk to me and how you take care of me."

They kissed one another before walking into the house.

♦ ♥ ♦ Royalty Crowned ♦ ♥ ♦

"Ma, have you talked to Ma Tanya?" Jasean asked over the phone.

"No, but she promised to bring the kids by for a while. I'm waiting for her to get here. And hello to you, too! I would pay to know how you're doing, son," Evelyn replied mockingly.

"I know I'm bothering you, but I miss my kids. What the hell was YaYa thinking pulling a gun on Endy and them? Yo, she really bugging!"

"I don't know what you did to that girl. Whatever it was, you have driven her completely insane."

"I know, Ma! I don't feel like hearing that shit right now, okay?"

"Well, alright. Just pray you at least won't be shipped too far so you can at least see your children."

"I'm praying every day that God keeps me close. I know Endy done moved on, but I at least wanted my kids to grow up near their father, you know?"

"Who is this man she's seeing? I heard he got money. Do you know him?" asked Evelyn.

"Yeah, it's the dude she dated when we split before. I heard she ran into him while she was in North Carolina."

He tried to act like he was unbothered, but deep down, it was killing him to know someone else was caring for, spending time with, and making love to the woman who had his heart ever since he was fifteen years old.

Ding, dong!

"That must be Tanya," said Evelyn as she raced to the door, anxious to see her grand-babies.

"Granny!" squealed Patience.

"Hi, Granny's baby! Say hello to your daddy," cooed Evelyn as she gave Patience the phone.

"Daddy!" yelled Patience.

"Hi, Daddy's princess. I miss you so much," whimpered Jasean at the sound of her voice.

Tanya handed Peace over to Evelyn and grabbed the phone from Patience.

"Let me speak to your daddy really quick, baby."

"Hey, Ma. How have you been?" Jasean stuttered.

"No need to be worried, son. My love for you didn't die with you and Endy's divorce. I love you just as before."

"Thanks, Ma. And thank you for bringing them by for a little while."

"My pleasure, sweetie. Well, I got to go, but you take care."

Tanya gave Evelyn the phone back.

Evelyn wrapped up the call with Jasean as Tanya got the children settled for their visit.

AFTER THE BETRAYAL

"Thanks so much for this, Tanya," Evelyn said.

"You don't have to thank me. I know you love these kids. Give me a kiss before I go, Patience."

"Ummmmwah," Patience poked out her little lips.

"She is just the most beautiful thing," remarked Evelyn as she beamed down at Patience.

"Yes, she is. Alright, see y'all later."

"I see somebody is happy!" said Marilyn, arriving just as Tanya was about to leave.

"I'm happy as hell right now. I missed my babies so much!"

Marilyn didn't want to ruin the moment with her news, but she needed to tell Evelyn what was going on with Jasean's case.

"I need to talk to you urgently."

"Uh oh, I don't like the sound of that. What's going on?" asked Evelyn.

"I spoke with Juan, and they are not able to locate the witness. He said even his FBI connect couldn't locate him."

"Oh, no! My baby can't go down for murder!" gasped Evelyn.

"Calm down. I have Matthew on it. We have to discuss the deal they wanted to give him."

"Oh, no, sis. This doesn't sound good. Damn it, Jay! I told them to leave that shit alone. Look, I can't deal with this today. I'm trying to enjoy my grandbabies. We will discuss this later."

Ding, dong!

"Are you expecting somebody?" Marilyn asked.

"No. Go see who it is," Evelyn replied as she sat on the floor with the children.

"Oh, Sally, how you doing? Hmm, where's Lil' Jay?" questioned Marilyn.

"I was hoping YaYa brought him here," Sally responded while walking in the house.

Evelyn jumped up from the floor. "What you mean? I thought he was under your care?"

"Ev, calm down. Now, Sally, what happened? Where's YaYa?" Marilyn asked.

"Niyana came by the house saying she wanted to turn herself in. But first, she wanted to take a shower, eat something, and spend a little time with us. Next thing I know, we all fell asleep, and when I woke up, she and Lil' Jay were gone," sobbed Sally.

"I know you're not saying she's on the run with my grandson..." Evelyn began to panic.

"Ev, I'm sorry, but she promised me that she would do the right thing. I was tired and fell asleep. When I woke up, she was gone. I swear I didn't think she would do something like that," explained Sally.

"Sally, the only thing we can do is call the police," Evelyn advised.

"Nooooo! I don't want that baby to get hurt because of YaYa's foolishness," retorted Sally hysterically.

"Sally, Ev is right," Marilyn interjected. "We have to let the cops know. They can hurt her onsite since she is titled armed and dangerous," explained Marilyn.

Sally hung her head and wept silently, feeling defeated.

"Alright, I guess we have no choice."

"I'm calling the police before we don't see my grandson no more," Evelyn said while picking up her phone to dial 911.

♦ ♥ ♦ Royalty Crowned ♦ ♥ ♦

Rich entered the bedroom and watched as Endy slept. He walked toward the bed and removed the covers so he could admire her sexy body. Then he gently turned her over and ever so lightly began to pamper her body with kisses. Feeling mischievous, Rich decided

149

to flick her clit with his tongue.

"Baby, what are you doing?" moaned Endy as she woke up.

"I want to watch the sunrise with you. I dreamed of the day I could do this with you," said Rich bashfully as he softly kissed her belly button, thighs, and each of her toes.

She just looked at him and smiled. He was such a romantic.

"Before we go watch the sunrise, I want to make you nut at least twice, though," Rich muttered as he dipped his tongue into his woman.

Within minutes, Rich had Endy squirming in the sheets and about to reach her first climax. Being a man of his word, he slid back in, not allowing Endy to recover. He needed to make her cum. He needed to know she was really here—really with him right now.

"Damn, baby," moaned Endy as she climaxed for a second time.

Certain that Endy would be weak, Rich scooped her up bridal-style and carried her outside. He cradled her body as night slowly turned into day. He was painfully hard as he held Endy's naked body close to his; his excitement was tenfold after not seeing her for a while. He could tell she was ready for him to be inside of her, so he adjusted her so that she straddled him.

"Ride me," Rich whispered as he planted gentle kisses on her body.

"With pleasure."

She lifted her body and slowly inserted his manhood inside her. With every inch that disappeared in her, Endy's moans got louder. When he had fully inserted all of him, she rolled her hips and grinded on him, knowing how it drove him crazy. Rich's eyes rolled back, and he let out a loud, throaty moan. He needed more. He grabbed her ass and began to thrust upward into her.

"I'm gonna bust, babe."

"Me too."

The sun's beams washed over them as they both climaxed.

After Rich caught his breath, he said, "I got something special for you today, baby. So, brace yourself!"

"I'm sure that whatever it is, I'm going to love it."

"Well, let's get dressed and let the festivities begin."

♦ ❤ ♦ RoyaltyCrowned ♦ ❤ ♦

It was Valentine's Day, and the crew indulged themselves in a slew of activities like jet-skiing, snorkeling, brunch, and a full spa day. Now it was time for their oceanside dinner.

Everyone came downstairs, looking and smelling like a million bucks. They were dressed like they were going to a black-tie event.

"Ladies and gentlemen, please follow me this way," said Juan as he directed the group toward the water.

Rose petals led to a canopy that had a table set for the lovely couples. White lights surrounded the area, setting off the most perfect and intimate mood.

Turning to Rich, Endy squealed and kissed him all over. "Baby! Oh, my goodness! This is so beautiful."

"I told you that I was going to make sure you had the best day ever. I loved you from the first time I saw you. When God blessed me with you again, I promised myself never to let you go," Rich earnestly said as he stroked her cheek.

"You all may be seated! Dinner will be served in a few," announced Felix.

There was a four course five-star type restaurant meal that included large lobsters and shrimp. Expensive wine and a band playing beautiful jazz and R&B music. The breeze was just right and not too windy. Endy was just so in awe at her surprise.

AFTER THE BETRAYAL

"I would like to make a toast," said Rich as he stood up, holding a champagne flute in his hand. "This day is about my baby and making her forget about everything in her past. Endyia, I loved you from the first day I laid eyes on you. I've watched you go from being broken to a boss-ass queen. You did it all on your own with courage, strength, and prayer. I told you I'm a patient man, but I can't wait to give you the world and everything you could ever dream of."

Rich kneeled on one knee.

"Babe, what are you doing?"

Endy's eyes pooled with tears.

"Something I should have done years ago," responded Rich, pulling out a platinum ring box from his jacket pocket.

"When I told you that I got you for life, I meant it. You, Patience, and Peace. Just give me a chance to show you."

He opened the lid of the box to reveal a ten-karat diamond ring.

"Baby, wow! I don't know what to say. You don't think this is too soon?" Endy asked anxiously, her rational mind kicking in.

"Endy, I got you, baby. I'm a patient man, so I will give you the time you need to make a decision. You don't have to give me an answer now. Just know you are my forever."

Hearing the sincerity in Rich's voice made Endy want to slap herself for questioning if they were moving too fast. Looking at this man and all he had done for her in such a short time touched her heart—especially when he referred to Patience and Peace as his children.

"Yes, babe. I will be your forever," shouted Endy as she jumped on him, wrapping her legs around his waist.

Everyone clapped and ran to them, yelling congratulations. Well, everyone besides Reeko and Tylon, who sat there pouting with their arms crossed. Endy felt the tension from them, but she was so overwhelmed with happiness that she wasn't going to let anyone ruin it for her.

"To me and my wife-to-be," Rich said as he held up his glass of champagne in a toast.

"Yes, baby, to us and our new life," Endy toasted.

AFTER THE BETRAYAL

SONG CRY

Chapter 19

When Endy and everyone arrived in Brooklyn, they heard about what happened and headed straight to Luella's house. Aunt Sally stayed the night there because she was too shaken up and worried. YaYa was now considered armed and dangerous, so Aunt Sally was scared of the potential outcomes.

"Auntie, what happened?"

Niema hugged Aunt Sally the moment she caught sight of her.

"Niyana came by the house. I was exhausted from dealing with the baby, so I dozed off. By the time I got up, she and the baby were gone. On top of everything, she's also facing kidnapping charges now."

"What?! She stole the baby?" Niema yelled frantically.

"Y'all, we have to find out where she's at and convince her to bring that baby back and turn herself in," Endy told them.

"How you suppose we do that?" Niema questioned.

"Oh, she is not getting far. The police are on the lookout for the truck, and it's all over the news. Best believe someone will be calling us soon," Aunt Sally replied.

"Yes, let's just be patient and let the police handle it. This some bullshit yo," Niema barked.

♦ ❤ ♦ RoyaltyCrowned ♦ ❤ ♦

Lil' Jay cried as hard and loud as his little lungs allowed.

"Baby, please stop crying. Mommy can't stop right now to feed you," YaYa cried in desperation.

Lil' Jay continued to scream, failing to understand why he wasn't being fed. YaYa could feel herself losing control, and she needed to get herself together.

"I'm going to call your grandma Evelyn."

"Hello?"

"It's me...YaYa."

"YaYa! Where the hell are you with my grandson?" screamed Evelyn.

"Don't pretend you care. Look, I need you to meet me so you can get him. I'm tired, Ev."

"Sure! Where are you? I'll come get him right now."

"Meet me at Aunt Sally's house."

"Okay, I'm on my way. Please be safe with the baby."

♦ ❤ ♦ RoyaltyCrowned ♦ ❤ ♦

As everyone arrived at Aunt Sally's house, they spotted YaYa's truck parked out front.

155

AFTER THE BETRAYAL

They could hear Lil' Jay screaming and crying. Evelyn jumped out of her truck and raced towards YaYa's vehicle. When Evelyn snatched the door open, YaYa drew her gun.

"YaYa, what the hell is wrong with you?" Evelyn barked.

"Niyana, put that damn gun away now," begged Aunt Sally, who was standing right behind Evelyn.

"He made me think we had something special. He made me think we could have a life together. Then he switched on me. He switched on me! I was good enough to sleep with but not good enough to be his girl," cried YaYa, tapping the gun to her head.

"Look, sweetheart, I'm sorry my son did this to you, but you have to pull yourself together. If not for you, do it for your baby," advised Evelyn.

"He switched on me! He switched on me!" YaYa bellowed.

"Niyana, stop this nonsense now. There are too many good men out here for you to chase a married one," rebuked Aunt Sally.

In the distance, police sirens could be heard approaching Aunt Sally's house. Panicking, YaYa started shuffling around the car. She knew it was all over for her. While YaYa was distracted with her thoughts, Evelyn grabbed Lil' Jay and ran back to her car.

"Niyana, get out and stand beside me. I don't want these pigs to shoot you, baby," shouted Aunt Sally.

"We need y'all to step away from the vehicle and get behind us. Y'all have three seconds," an officer yelled into his bullhorn.

YaYa was about to step out until she realized she would never see her son again. If she couldn't see her son anymore, she was better off dead.

The police carefully walked toward her vehicle, and before she could react, they grabbed hold of her and attempted to drag her out of the truck while she still held tight to the gun.

"Fuck y'all, pigs! Y'all gonna have to kill me today," ranted YaYa as she struggled with the police officers.

Boom!

A shot was fired in the vehicle. YaYa continued to struggle until she caught a glimpse of Lil' Jay in Evelyn's arms, and for a second, everything went still. If she died right in that moment, she would never see his precious face again. At least being in jail, she could see photos of him or even see him during visitation hours. YaYa fell limp and finally allowed the officers to pull her out of the truck and onto the ground.

AFTER THE BETRAYAL

MONEY AIN'T A THING

Chapter 20

Endy looked at her phone and saw it was fifteen minutes past the designated meeting time.

"Yo, where the hell is Nina?"

"Baby, calm down. Why are you so on edge?" Tanya asked.

"I got to get the fuck out of New York with my babies."

There was a knock at the door.

"That must be Nina," said Endy, rushing to the door.

"I'm sorry I'm late. I got caught up with something. Now, before we do this, I want to make sure you understand that it's done. Once you sign, everything is solely yours," Nina explained as she laid out all the documents.

"Yes, I'm sure. I'm ready."

"Okay. Well, let's get this show on the road."

Endy signed the papers that gave her power of attorney over everything. Nina pulled out a bottle of champagne from her bag and popped the cork. All the properties, businesses, assets, and savings were now solely owned by Endy. She had officially become a multi-millionaire in her own right.

"Ma, I need all the family to meet me at Nana's this evening. I want to share the good news."

"You and your children's future are about to be very bright after this last deal closes," Nina told her.

She and Endy sat down and went through the remaining paperwork. Endy was determined not to give up, ensuring she and the children were set for life.

♦ ❤ ♦ RoyaltyCrowned ♦ ❤ ♦

"Chynna, you sure you don't know what this meeting is about?" Lisa asked her daughter as she drove.

"No, Ma! I just know Aunt Tanya said Endy wanted to meet with the whole family," Chynna replied.

"Where's Asia? Her tail has been MIA lately," Lisa questioned.

"You know Asia is bipolar as hell. She feels like Endy gets all the attention anyway," Chynna laughed.

"Yeah, I think all you bitches are bipolar," Keisha said, also laughing.

"Whoa! I see all the gang is here," Chynna commented as she pulled up to Luella's.

"Hello, everyone. Aunt Linda, Thee, I didn't know y'all were here, too." Lisa ran over and hugged them.

"It's supposed to be spring, and it feels like winter up here. I don't miss this mess at all," Aunt Linda complained.

"Where's your child? She called this family meeting, and she's late!" Keisha nagged.

AFTER THE BETRAYAL

"I'm right here! What's good, fambam?" Endy came in all hyped.

All the family was in attendance and seated in the living room. Endy was ready to tell her good news. She knew some wouldn't be happy for her, but she didn't care. Either they were in, or they were out—she wasn't wasting any time.

"Since everyone is here, I'm going to get straight to the point. As you all know, I have transitioned down South to start my new life. I know many of you aren't happy about it, but I have some things to discuss with you. First, I sold the club property and our house. I did that so I could buy three other properties located in midtown and downtown Brooklyn. I'm expanding E-Class and opening an office building. The other property is a condo for me to stay at while I'm in town and rent to people in town on business when I am not staying there. I know Jay is not going to be happy about my decision to close the club and sell the property, but whatever. My divorce was finalized a few months ago, so I've been on go mode ever since. This is why I've been MIA lately, going back and forth to Carolina. I put a lot of the money in stocks and investments. I had to make sure my kids and me are financially stable. I worked too hard for what I have. I wasn't about to let Jay's nonsense mess up me and my children's futures."

"Wait a minute. So, you sold your house and the club? Who's going to run E-Class while you're gone? Why an office building?" Tanya asked without pausing to take a breath.

"I'm getting to that, Mommy. I'm going to let Rizzy be part-owner of the E-Class brand. Then I'm going to invest in her clothing and cosmetics line," Endy continued.

"Whoa! What? Oh my God! Cuz, thank you so much." Karishma jumped up from the sofa and hugged her tight.

"What is the point of all of us being here, baby?" Luella asked.

"I'm starting a marketing and promotion company as a family business. We'll promote and market businesses all around the world. Now, whoever wants to be part of this will have to take it seriously. It's a lot of work going into this, so I need everyone to give their all with this project."

"Count me in. I've been wanting to put my business degree to use," Chynna said.

"I was getting to that. Chynna, I need you to do all the paperwork and bookkeeping. Egypt will be in charge of the clients. Our public relations rep, Asia, can be in control of the media marking, and J.J. and Lynasia will be in charge of all the marketing and promotions. So, what do y'all think?" Endy asked her family.

"I love it! With technology on the rise, this will be a great opportunity for the whole family. We will build a foundation for the kids!" Chynna said encouragingly.

"Baby girl, that's very smart, and to include your family was genius. Because who can you trust more than your cousins?" Tanya asked rhetorically and hugged her.

"Well, I'm about to make some moves. I'm meeting Ny at the hospital. She's there with YaYa."

"Okay, just keep me posted on the next steps, boo," Chynna said.

"Bet. Talk to y'all later," Endy said, then flew out the door.

CAN'T BELIEVE

Chapter 21

"I'm here to see Jasean Newman," Endy told the clerk when she arrived at the MDC Brooklyn Detention Center.

"Okay, ma'am. Please come right this way," the short lady guard told her.

They escorted her to the visiting area after she checked in the facility. She already decided that she wasn't going to visit again after that day. As she waited for Jasean to come to the visit, she gathered her thoughts on how she would tell him everything. A couple of minutes later, he entered the visiting area. She took a deep breath and prepared to tell the man she once loved that she was done completely.

"What's good, ma? Can I have a hug?" Jasean asked, eyeing her up and down.

Endy reluctantly hugged him. She figured since it was probably the last time, she would ever see him, she could grant him that one desire. It didn't help him that she looked good and smelled delicious. She sported light blue jeans she ordered from Fashion Nova, a black fitted T-shirt, a pair of black Chanel sneakers, and a purse to match. Her black leather jacket had bling on it from her boutique. Endy's stomach was on flat, and her ass was on fat. He literally started drooling when he saw her. She knew he would probably be upset that she didn't bring the kids. She didn't know how the visit would go, so she decided not to.

"I didn't bring the kids because it's too much to go through. Peace needs his bottles and food. I just want us to deal with the matter at hand, which is me moving to North Carolina," Endy said, straight to the point.

"Okay, Endy. I already know you're moving. Come on, you know I got eyes and ears in the streets. I begged for your forgiveness, so I don't know what else to do," Jasean replied, weary of the whole situation.

"There's nothing else to do but accept it and move on. I forgave you already."

"Yeah, the divorce is final, but we're not. I need to see my kids. I don't expect you to bring them, but at least let Mommy bring them."

"Jay, that's something I will consider. I just came to let you know I'm getting married. I sold the house, the club, and expanded E-Class. I'm also starting a marketing and pro-motion company in midtown. I will leave some money with Ma Ev for your lawyer fees, but I had to make sure me and the kids were straight. Even Lil' Jay," Endy told him.

"What the fuck you mean you will leave me some money? All that shit is mine. I helped you build E-Class. If you think you're going to take my money and go to Carolina to live it up with another dude, you got me fucked up!" Jasean jumped up.

"Aye, settle down!" a tall, slim male guard yelled.

"My bad, Cortez." Jasean threw his hand up as if surrendering.

"I don't have time for this shit. I'm trying to get my life back in order because you broke me down to nothing. I rebuilt myself while you were trying to figure shit out, Jay. I'm happy with my life right now. At least he gives me a sense of peace and has his own money," Endy barked back.

"What you mean you happy now? I know you not really serious about this Rich clown.

AFTER THE BETRAYAL

Come on, E! He ain't me!"

"I know he's not you! That's exactly why I fell in love with him! He's not going to hurt me, belittle me, cheat, lie, or choose the streets over his family! He's a real man, not a mama's boy! I'm going to marry him and have a real life!" Endy spat.

"Endy, really?! You really about to marry this clown and take my kids away from me?!"

"Aye, Newman! I told you to settle down. Don't make me cut your visit short," Cortez hollered.

"Jay, are you really mad right now? Dude, you fucked my best friend's cousin and had a baby with her. Are you kidding me right now, motherfucker?"

Cortez shot her a disapproving look, but Jasean sat in silence. Guilt wore his face because he knew he was dead wrong. There was no denying it. He couldn't say shit to defend himself. He was disloyal to his wife and brought on the deceit. He was still in love with her, but he knew it was over for them. There was no turning back now. All he could do was salvage the relationship with his kids at this point.

"Endy, come on. I was coked up, overworked, and dumb to mess up with you. I swear I didn't mean for shit to go that far. Please don't do this, man. Don't marry dude. At least take your time. I will forever regret losing the best woman I had," Jasean expressed, his voice trembling.

"Jay, it's over! I just wanted to be dignified enough to tell you in person. I'm leaving for North Carolina in a couple of days. Once I have the grand opening of E-Class Midtown, I won't be back in New York for a while."

"How am I supposed to see the kids?" Jasean questioned.

"We will work something out. Oh, since YaYa will be going to prison when she leaves the hospital, I'm taking Lil' Jay with me to Carolina. I think it would be good for him to be around his siblings. Plus, Ny is down there, and we'll be helping each other out with the kids."

"You got shit all figured out! Go be with that lame-ass clown! I'm telling you I'm coming for my kids once all this shit is over. You done took all I have! Fuck you, Endy! Fuck you!" he screamed.

The guards quickly came and apprehended him. Endy smirked as she stood up to leave. Her mission was accomplished. She wanted him to feel the hurt she once felt.

"No, no, no, no! Endy, come on! Just talk to me, baby! Endy, don't do this, damn it!" Jasean yelled as the guards hauled him away.

"Ha, ha, ha. Take that bastard. After all you put me through, you really think I owe you an explanation? Goodbye, Jasean Newman!"

Endy giggled to herself as she left the prison with her shades on and no plans to ever return.

Endy traveled the belt parkway to get to Tanya's house and pick up the kids. She weaved in and out of traffic, blasting T.I.'s If It Ain't About the Money. She felt relieved that everything was about to change for the better. Things finally felt like they were about to go her way.

After about her forty five minute drive, she arrived at Tanya's building. She jumped out of her new Benz and headed straight toward the elevator. Once she reached Tanya's condo, she perceived the smell of homemade lasagna seeping from underneath the door.

"Who is it?" Tanya yelled as Endy knocked persistently.

"It's your gorgeous daughter!"

"Girl, you better stop driving like a bat out of hell. There's no way you made it here that fast," Tanya grilled her.

"Ma, come on. Stop it! There was no traffic like that. I'm tired and have so much to do before the grand opening."

Endy kissed her cheek.

"And what's this I hear about you taking Lil' Jay with you down South?"

AFTER THE BETRAYAL

"Yes, Ma, I'm taking him. I think it's for the best since YaYa is going to prison. Where's the kids?"

"You know where they're at...in there with your dad watching TV like always. They take over my room when they come over here," Tanya laughed.

"Y'all got they asses spoiled. They not doing that with me. I'm teaching they butt early to sleep in their own beds."

"So why you dress all cute to see your ex?"

"I know, right? But I love this T-shirt and these sneakers from Chanel. I had to set it off with the jacket and purse. You know I had let him see what he lost," Endy said and winked arrogantly. "You know down South they don't even care about labels."

"They sure don't, but I'm glad you closed that Chapter with Jay. I told you eventually you will see it's not about revenge but more about closure. I'm also very happy for you and Rich. I love him for you and the kids," Tanya said in a more serious tone.

"Thanks for all the love and support, Mommy."

"Okay, so when can we get on with the plans for the wedding? I'm hoping for a spring or summer wedding. I can see you really love Rich, baby girl."

"Mommy, I love him very much. I won't deal with an unfaithful man. I deserved better. Fuck that. Jay messed up—not me. Rich came at the perfect time and swept me off my feet."

"Well, then...I'm ready to plan this million-dollar wedding," Tanya said, hugging her baby.

Endy scrunched up her face. "Ma, I think not. I'd rather we have something small and intimate. Where are my babies? I have to get a move on it."

"Okay, get your rug rats and speak to your father before you leave. You know he will catch a fit if you don't. Let me check on the garlic bread," Tanya said and hurried to the kitchen.

Endy headed back to her parent's bedroom, where she could hear the kids' favorite TV show playing.

"Hi, Daddy. I'm here to collect my munchkins," Endy sang as she entered the room.

"Hi, baby! I thought I heard you. I wasn't ready for them to go yet."

"I know, Daddy, but I have things to do before the grand opening in midtown. They will be back in two days. I just need to get them to their doctor appointments."

"Do you think it's healthy taking them back and forth? I don't know why you won't let me and Mommy keep them until you're settled. Now you're talking about taking in your ex-husband's bastard child. What's wrong with you, child?" Eddie asked in confusion.

"Nothing is wrong with me. That child did not ask to be here, and Ny will be helping me. I would let them stay with y'all, but my kids are my responsibility. Once I'm done with the grand opening of the store and marketing firm, I can take some time off. Then I can focus on my home, being a mother, and marrying a real man," Endy explained.

"Well, your mind is already made up. I apologize sweetheart. I want you to know we have your back. I love spending time with them, that's all."

"I understand, Daddy. I know y'all not happy about me moving down South, but it's better for the kids. I want to raise them in a better environment than Brooklyn. I want to start over in a new place and have a happy life. I will visit, but my time is up in New York."

"I know, baby. Maybe that will push your mother to go down South. I sure as hell want to move when I retire," Eddie laughed.

"Well, let's work on her, but until then, I will visit as much as I can," Endy said, then kissed his cheek.

He hugged her tight and kissed her forehead as if it were the last time, he would see her. Eddie loved his daughter and admired her independence.

"Baby girl, be careful and watch your surroundings. People are treacherous out here, and I don't trust them Newmans."

AFTER THE BETRAYAL

"I know, Daddy, believe me. I carry my pistol with me everywhere I go. I'm not going to let them catch me slipping," Endy reassured him.

"Okay, baby...as long as you're alert at all times. I'm not worried about you; it's them. Hell, I've been taking you to the range ever since you were six years old," Eddie said, chuckling.

"You're crazy, Daddy! I'm good. Ny is meeting me at the condo. We leave in the morning."

Eddie nodded and smiled lovingly.

"Ma, I'm gone! Your husband tried to kidnap my children. We will be back in a couple of days," Endy said, kissing her goodbye.

"Girl, you know I'm walking you downstairs," Eddie told her as he struggled to get up.

After another hug goodbye, Endy left her parents' house and was on her way to meet Ny.

"Yo, where you at?" she shouted into the phone.

"I'm on my way to your crib," Niema told her. "I just got Aunt Sally situated. I picked up Lil' Jay and Nasim, so I will be there soon. Hmm, I think this calls for some wine," Niema added teasingly.

"Yes, let's get it, boo," Endy cheered.

"Bitch, bye," Niema laughed and hung up.

Endy finally arrived at the condo. After getting the children settled while she waited for Niema.

Her condo was on point. It was located on the 12th floor, so she had a great view of New York City. It was beautifully decorated and very spacious. She lit some candles, put on some 90s R&B music, ordered them some takeout, and sat down on her suede sofa to stare out her big bay windows. She already reserved the car service to transport them to the airport in the morning. She just wanted to enjoy her view and some laughs with her friend.

There was a knock at the door.

Dang, Ny! You got here quick.

However, when she looked out the peephole, she didn't see anyone. She went to sit back down, and then the doorbell rang.

Who the fuck is that?

Endy grabbed her 9mm out of her purse.

She looked through the peephole again, but again, no one was there. She snatched open the door with the gun in her hand. Still, no one was there. She checked every area of her vicinity. Nothing. As she headed back inside, she could hear someone behind her, but it was too late to react because they assaulted her and rushed her inside the condo. She fell to the floor, dropping the gun in the process.

"You better leave my husband alone!" the woman yelled repetitively while attacking her.

Endy managed to fight off the woman and grab her gun off the floor. She shot a few bullets erratically without aiming, attempting to scare off the hysterical woman.

"Where you going, you fucking coward?! If you wanna scare me, why the hell you running?"

Endy immediately jumped up when she heard the kids crying. She grabbed her cell phone off the bar counter and raced to lock the door. She then headed back to the room to check on them and dialed 911 and her parents.

The police arrived within a few minutes, along with her parents. She didn't want to call too many of her family members, especially since she was okay.

"Oh my God! Endy! What the fuck? Where's Endy? Endy? Endy, are you okay?!" Niema yelled as she raced through the condo.

"Ny, I'm right here," Endy said as she stood talking to one of the policemen.

AFTER THE BETRAYAL

"Oh, my goodness. What the hell happened? Why are the cops here?" Niema cried.

"Girl, some chick dressed in black and a mask came here and threatened me to leave her husband alone. I didn't tell nobody that part, though. I need to speak with Rich first. I did shoot at whoever it was, and I think I hit her."

"Well, well, well, what do we have here? Mrs. Newman, I guess y'all don't get enough of me, huh?" Officer Clay stated in a sarcastic tone.

"Yo, are you the only cop in New York? I need y'all to get this bitch, or I will. If it wasn't for her sneaking me, y'all would be calling the coroner instead," Endy spat.

"Well, good thing, because your babies don't need both parents in prison."

"Yo, arrest the bitch that attacked me. Just take my statement and get the hell out of my house!" Endy yelled at him.

"Baby girl, chill. He wants you to act up. Don't give them a reason to mess with you," Tanya told her.

"Mommy, this is crazy! Why aren't they out looking for her?!" Endy screamed.

"Do you know why this woman would come here to attack you?" Officer Warren asked.

"No. I don't even know the woman. She rushed me, we tussled, and I shot. That's it."

"Wow. And you haven't had any problems with anyone but Ms. Bradley?" Officer Clay asked.

"I told you no. Now, are y'all going to look for her or not?" Endy snapped.

"Aye," Officer Clay said and threw his hands up as if to tell her to chill. "Mrs. Newman, you need to come with us to the station."

"I just can't escape this fucking nonsense up here. I'm so ready to blow New York and move down South," Endy cried.

"Baby, it's alright. We will be there after we get the kids settled," Tanya reassured her, pained at what her child was going through.

"Damn, Endy. I'm right behind you, and Rich is on his way," Niema told her.

Endy went to the station to give a statement, which took a couple of hours. She then shot straight to Luella's afterwards to see her children. Rich called to let her know he would meet her there. Her main concern was her children and making sure they were okay.

"Cuz, are you okay? Who the hell is trying to mess with you?" Chynna bombarded her with questions as Endy walked into Luella's house.

"I don't know who this chick is, but I'm about to find out," Endy ranted.

"Where's Rich? Does he know what's going on?" Chynna asked.

"Yes, and he's livid, girl. He should be here any minute," Endy replied.

Before she could fully finish her statement, he came rushing into the house.

"Baby, are you okay?"

Rich raced over and embraced Endy.

"Yes, baby, I'm okay. I was worried about the kids mostly. You know I had me covered. Aye, I need to speak to you alone."

When they walked toward the den in silence, Rich knew it couldn't be good.

"So why was I attacked by a woman who told me to leave her husband alone? Are you married, Rich?"

Endy's nose flared.

"Not no more," he replied. "But I do need to tell you some things about my ex-wife. If you don't want to get married after that, I understand. Please just give me a chance to explain."

"Fuck, Rich! What is it?"

AFTER THE BETRAYAL

PAPERS

Chapter 22

"Yo, I need you to chill. Do you need us to help you with anything as far as the grand opening?" Chynna asked Endy.

"Yes, I'm ready to party. YaYa is doing better, so I can finally breathe," Niema added.

"Well, since y'all offered, I do need help to pull this relaunch off. I got a few loose ends to tie up," Endy said with a head full of rollers.

The girls were all in rollers, lounge clothes, and full makeup, preparing for Karishma's grand opening of the midtown store.

"So, what do you need us to do?" Chynna asked.

"Can you make sure the caterers set up everything right? Just oversee what they are doing," Endy replied.

"Okay, got you," Chynna said and nodded affirmatively.

"Do you need me to do anything?" Niema offered.

"If you don't mind, can you go down to Party City on Nostrand or Atlantic Avenue and pick up the balloons for me? That will just leave me the DJ, party planner, and the inventory. Oh, of course, I want y'all to wear some E-Class originals," Endy told them.

"Hell yeah, girl! I would be honored. Aye, I want to thank y'all for all the support y'all showed me and my family," Niema expressed, getting emotional.

"Everybody deserves a second chance. Besides, YaYa was never the issue. Jay was the person who owed me loyalty," Endy told her.

Endy's phone rang, interrupting their heart-to-heart.

"Are you serious right now? I'm on my way," Endy said, then hung up.

"What's wrong? Why you looking like that?" Chynna asked in concern.

"That was Rizzy. It seems the feds are at E-Class. I need to go show proof that the property is hers. I guess they want to make sure Jay has no connection to the store. I just can't shake this dude or his nonsense," Endy groaned.

"How do they even know about the store?" Niema questioned.

"I don't know. I mean, nobody knew about this but family, so someone is a freaking rat. I'm going to find out who it is because right now is not the time for bullshit. I need this party to run as smoothly as possible. Aunt Karim is already skeptical about Rizzy running the store. I switched the business and everything under Rizzy's name so there won't be no nonsense."

"Well, let's get over there to see what the hell is going on. I'm right behind you, cuz. I'm gonna drop Enrique off at Reeko's mother's house," Chynna said as she picked up her son.

"Okay, meet me at the store, y'all. I'm out. This grand opening will not be ruined," Endy said as she raced out the door.

Niema and Chynna stood in shock because Endy had been through enough.

"Girl, them Newmans will mess up something. Damn!" Niema said, aggravated.

"Girl, y'all all tied to them people. Lord knows I'm glad it's not me, because I would be in jail by now," Chynna chuckled.

I know it, but your cousin changed all that for me. If I knew then what I know now about Roc, I would have let CJ's sorry ass go a long time ago," Niema laughed.

"Girl, come on. I don't want to hear all that. Let's go and see what's going on at the store," Chynna said, brushing her off.

They both headed out to drop off Chynna's son and meet Endy at the store.

Meanwhile, Endy booked it to midtown to see what was going on. Why were the feds at the boutique? When she finally got there, she saw the police car and her aunt Karim's car outside. Endy knew she was about to hear it from her aunt. She jumped out of the car and raced straight inside. As she entered the store, she saw an officer talking to her aunt.

"Hi, ma'am. I'm Agent Baker," the FBI agent said.

"Not y'all two again! What the hell are y'all doing here?" Endy spat.

Endy was familiar with Agents Baker and Jones because they were the same ones who arrested Jasean before. They had been following her and questioning people who knew her and the family.

"Endy! What the hell is going on? I told you I don't want Rizzy in none of y'all bullshit," Karim screamed at Endy.

"Auntie, this some bullshit. I would never put Rizzy in harm's way," Endy explained.

"Mommy, chill. I told you this is some hating shit. This is not her fault," Karishma argued.

"Auntie, you know damn well I would never put Rizzy in nonsense. This has the feds written all over it. They can't tie me to shit that has to do with Jay, period."

"Ma'am, I'm Officer Jones. We're here to follow up on a tip from a federal witness. They have connected this establishment with the drugs and money-laundering ring your husband was involved in."

"I don't give a fuck what type of tip y'all were given! The deed is under my cousin's name! She owns this building, so why are y'all here? I was exonerated of all charges! Stop messing with me before I go to your boss! I'm no longer married to him, so leave me alone," Endy fumed.

"Sorry, I think there was a bit of a misunderstanding, Mrs. Newman," Officer Baker replied.

"First of all, I'm not Mrs. Newman no more. I'm Ms. Hinton. Secondly, we have a grand opening in the next few hours. So, I would appreciate it if you went about your way because y'all being here doesn't look good for business!" Endy yelled.

"Sorry for the inconvenience," Agent Baker expressed again as they walked away.

"I know this asshole didn't just smirk," Karim groaned.

"Mommy, please calm down. Just let them go," Karishma pleaded with her.

"I told you I don't want you involved in any of this bullshit they got going on," she said, darting her eyes at Endy.

"Aunt Karim, I promise you this was a mistake. Jay got picked up on some more charges, and they're trying to tie me to it," Endy explained.

"I'm going to say this once. I don't want my child in no mess at all. She worked too hard to get through school to get caught up in any illegal crap."

Karim stormed off furiously as Chynna and Niema walked in. Endy knew someone tried to set her up.

Endy teared up. "I promise you cousin, I would never put you in any nonsense. I want to give the family a new start."

"I know that, cuz. Just let Mommy calm down. You know how she is with stuff like this. Ever since they did what they did to Grandad, she doesn't trust cops," Karishma reminded her.

Years ago, in Selma, North Carolina, Endy's grandfather RJ—short for Rodney James— was killed by a white racist cop. He was shot in front of his wife and children. Luella couldn't bear the grief of losing her husband at such a young age, so she took her children to New York and never looked back.

"I know. My mom still gets angry about it, too," Endy added.

"We still have a grand opening to do, y'all! Now, we not going to let one monkey stop the show, are we?" Chynna said, interrupting them before it got emotional.

"No. You're right. We got this. I love y'all so much. Thanks for always having my back." Endy hugged her cousins.

"Babe, I got you. Aunt Karim did let y'all asses have it, though," Chynna laughed.

"You so stupid, yo!" Niema laughed at Chynna's comment.

"Okay, let's get to work. I'm going to check the inventory," Endy said, pulling it together.

"I guess the party is on. Everything is okay. We got it handled, you guys," Karishma informed the party planners, who looked uneasy.

A few hours later, the ladies were dressed, the place was beautifully decorated, and the food layout was exquisite. It was ribbon-cutting time, and everyone was extremely excited for Karishma. She looked beautiful in her black satin, halter mermaid gown. Endy donned a black gown that was low-cut in the back, fitting all her curves. Both ladies had their hair styled into curls, and their makeup was naturally flawless. Rich couldn't keep his eyes off Endy. People could see how happy the two of them were.

"Girl, why you sitting over here with that sad look on your face? Everything worked out. Everybody's having fun," Ari said, startling Endy out of her deep thoughts.

"I know, but I don't want nothing popping off," Endy explained.

"Girl, have some fun. Everything is good, babe. Look around. You did it! You opened the biggest boutique in midtown. It's time to celebrate," Ari reminded her.

"You're right. Let's go get a drink and dance before my feet start hurting," Endy laughed.

The deejay was rocking the crowd. Everything was perfect, but Endy couldn't help but see Rich in a heated discussion with a Hispanic woman at the bar. Right when she was about to approach them, she ran into her mother.

"Endy! Hi, baby. We're about to go. Your grandmother is tired," Tanya told her.

"Okay, Mommy, that's fine. We'll be shutting down in a couple of hours. Where's Nana anyway?" Endy asked, noticing Rich and the woman had disappeared.

"She is saying goodbye to everyone. Are you okay? You look like something is wrong," Tanya questioned her.

"Hi, baby. We're about to go," Luella said, interrupting their conversation.

"Oh, no! Mommy, I'm good. Just a little tired, that's all. I'm glad y'all had a good time."

"Yes, I did, baby. Y'all did that," Luella agreed.

"Let me walk y'all outside," Endy said as she grabbed her grandmother's hand.

When the valet brought Tanya's car around, she and Luella quickly jumped in due to the cold. Endy kissed them both and said her goodbyes. She was about to head back into the store, but in her peripheral vision, she sensed someone staring at her. She looked to her left, and it was the same Hispanic woman who had been talking to Rich. The woman smirked and walked off. Endy knew she had to be someone he knew.

"Girl, why are you out here? It's cold. Are you okay?" Chynna asked her.

"Yeah, I'm good, but I need to have a conversation with Mr. Richmond right quick. I saw him and some chick having a heated convo inside. I think it's his ex," Endy griped.

"Girl, what you talking about 'a heated convo'? Why would his ex-come here?"

"He had told me his ex has been popping up. I have a feeling that was her, and I also think she was the one who came to my condo."

"Oh, hell no! You need to see what the hell is up. I didn't know all this was going on, cuz. Why didn't you tell me? Where the hell did, she go?" Chynna asked, looking around.

"Yeah, I'm about to talk to him right now. This hoe definitely won't be comfortable just popping up to shit," Endy said, then stormed inside.

Spotting Rich, she walked over to talk to him.

"Hello, my handsome husband-to-be. Can I speak to you for a minute?" Endy flashed a fake smile to him and some colleagues he invited.

"Sure, my queen. Excuse me, I will be right back," he told his colleagues. Once they got a distance away, Rich asked her, "Ma, are you okay?"

"That depends on what your answer to this question is," Endy snapped.

"Oh, shit! Am I in trouble or something?"

"'Oh, shit' is right! Who was the chick you were in a heated discussion with at the bar?"

"Damn! I didn't know you saw that. That was Maribel Perez, my ex-wife. I don't know how she knew about the grand-opening party for the store, but believe me, you have nothing to worry about."

"Your ex-wife Maribel? Why the hell was she here? Is she the one who came to my condo? Why didn't you tell me?! I would have called the police!"

"I know, babe. I don't know how she found out your information. Her ass tried to renege on signing the paperwork because she knows about our engagement. She claims it wasn't her who came to your house, and she has an alibi. She will bury herself soon, believe me. She gets too damn messy when her illness kicks in. My people are on it."

"Why would she be worried about us? I thought y'all marriage was strictly business for the last couple of years anyhow?"

"Because she wants to be spiteful now. She knew we had a business relationship, but now she wants to play like it was more. Don't worry, ma, that bitch knows not to mess with me. I got this handled. You and the kids are my top priority. I promise you that," Rich reassured her.

"We have to get her to sign those papers, Rich. The wedding is coming up. So, whatever you need to do to handle it, do it. Because you don't want me to have to do it,"

AFTER THE BETRAYAL

Endy advised him.

"No, I don't, ma. She's going to sign those papers one way or another. I appreciate you for understanding, babe. I promise you I will not do anything to jeopardize our union," Rich said and leaned in for a kiss.

"Yeah, I understand, but she better know who's the head bitch in charge. Tell her the next time she tries to attack me, my bullet won't miss," Endy barked and walked away.

Damn, that was sexy as hell. I love that girl, Rich thought to himself and smiled, fascinated by her feisty attitude.

Endy grabbed Karishma and headed to the deejay booth. Maribel had thrown Endy off guard, and she wanted to close out the party.

"Hi, y'all! I just want to say thanks to everyone who came out to celebrate with me. The grand opening was a success, and I'm extremely excited for the future of E-Class. As we close out this night, I want to shout out my cousin, Endyia, who believed in my vision and invested in my dream. I love you, cousin," Karishma said and passed the microphone to Endy.

"I'm so proud of you, Rizzy! You did everything I asked you to do and with no problem. I have no doubt that you will run E-Class smoothly. You deserve all the success coming your way," Endy said, then hugged her as the crowd clapped and cheered loudly.

"Okay, well, let's get this place cleaned up. Hell, I have to be back here in the morning. We'll talk before you leave," Karishma whispered to Endy.

After the store was cleaned and set up for the next day of business, they all left. Endy and Rich headed to their penthouse in New Jersey. They both showered and got comfortable as they sat on their heated balcony. He tried to get touchy-feely with her, but Endy wasn't feeling it—she was still upset about Maribel.

"Rich, I'm not playing with you. I'm gonna let you do this on your own, but if you can't handle this bitch, then I will. She will not get away with attacking me either. I'm going to bed. See you in the morning."

Damn, Maribel...your trifling ass won't mess up my happiness. That's a promise, Rich swore as he downed his glass of Henny.

DON'T YOU MESS WITH MY MAN

Chapter 23

Endy and Rich finally settled into their new home and were preparing for Thanksgiving. They hadn't been back in New York for a couple of months, and they weren't pressed to rush back either. The South was the change of scenery they both needed.

"I'm so excited that our parents will be here for Thanksgiving!" Endy exclaimed.

"I know, baby. This is going to be one of the best I've had in years. I rarely spent holidays with my family. Hell, I was always gone for work most times."

"Well, that's all gonna change when we get married. I'm big on spending time with family, especially during the holidays. I don't care if it's just me, you, and the kids. We will do holidays together," Endy remarked.

"I know, babe. This is what I always wanted. You're my dream come true, and I don't just say that shit to be saying it. I mean it with every part of my soul. You're my sunshine on a cloudy day," whispered Rich, then nipped her ear while running his hands down her body.

"Okay, stop it before you get something started," flushed Endy as she moved away.

"I'm not opposed to a quickie," Rich stated, licking his lips and wiggling his eyebrows.

"Boy, let me get to the supermarket to get my ingredients. Everyone will be here in a little bit, so let me go! You got Peace and Lil' Jay, babe, but I'm taking Patience with me."

"I got this. Go ahead to the market."

"Okay, I'll be back soon. Their snacks and drinks are already prepared, babe."

Endy had half an hour to make it to the seafood market on Capital Boulevard. Endy's parents loved fried fish during the holidays, so she wanted to prepare them a feast to their liking.

As Endy walked through the aisles, she kept catching a glimpse of a woman. The woman would appear in the aisle before her or after her.

After a few awkward and intentional encounters, Endy approached her angrily and asked, "Are you following me?"

The woman giggled. "There's no need to be hostile. Do you even know who I am?"

"I do. And, sweetie, I don't really care what you and Rich had going on. Don't you ever approach me in any manner with my child present. I will molly wop your ass in this store," hissed Endy.

"Honey, I don't fight. I'm far too pretty for that bullshit," Maribel responded, laughing as she walked away.

"Bitch your lucky I have my daughter with me I'll see you soon though," She yelled as Maribel headed out the Food Lion.

◆ ❤ ◆ Royalty Crowned ◆ ❤ ◆

Rich knew something was wrong with Endy. She hadn't spoken to him since she got back from the supermarket. She was very snappy and short with him. Their parents and family had arrived, and he was happy to host their first family dinner together.

"So, Endyia, how are the kids doing with daycare? Shoot, in my days, the women kept the kids home and tended to the house while the men worked. I guess nowadays you young girls are chasing your dreams," Rich's mother, Patricia, said.

"Oh, Ma, they're doing just fine at daycare. I'm not really the domestic type. I like to make my own money," Endy calmly replied, not rising to the bait.

Sensing the tension, Rich quickly changed the subject.

"Mr. Eddie, are you looking forward to retiring?"

"Yes. The property you found for us in Florida is beautiful. We will be there for a few weeks. I need to get away from that cold weather for a while."

"I know that's right. Endy and I sure will be down for a visit soon," Rich laughed, immediately going silent when he spotted Endy rolling her eyes.

"Endy, are you okay? You haven't been talking that much. You were full of excitement earlier on the phone. Now you just seem bothered or something. Are you sure you're, okay?" whispered Niema as she walked over to Endy.

"I'm good. Just a little tired from all that cooking," Endy lied.

"You got it done, baby girl, so I commend you," said Tanya, raising her glass towards Endy.

"I know that had to be hard since you don't cook much or at all," remarked Patricia.

"Ma, don't do that. Endy cooks all the time," Rich said, admonishing his mother.

Endy smirked at how he defended her but gave him an indifferent look.

Rich was hoping it won him some brownie points with Endy, but before he could go and ask, his phone vibrated from a text message. He didn't want to pull it out at the table and seem rude. So, instead, he excused himself to the kitchen to see who had texted him.

When he finally looked at his phone, he was shocked at what was sent.

Yeah, I told your ass you're not going to get away from me that easy. So, either you get rid of her, or I will. Your stepdaughter looked so cute today at the market. Me and Ms. Endyia had a very nice talk. LOL! Hope you're enjoying your Thanksgiving.

Attached to the message were multiple photos of Endy and Patience, who were oblivious they were being photographed at the store.

"What the fuck?" groaned Rich.

At least now I know why she's upset, he thought.

"I have let you disrespect me in my house too many times!"

Endy's scream reached the kitchen, interrupting his train of thought.

Rich rushed back into the dining room, only to pass Endy making her way out.

"What the hell is going on?"

"Your mother is being disrespectful to my parents and me."

"Momma, chill with that bullshit, would you?! I told you Endy is everything I want and need her to be, not you," Rich hissed as he went after Endy.

Rich found Endy in their bedroom on the balcony.

"Rich, what's the deal with you and Maribel? I don't have time for any setbacks."

"Please calm down and tell me what she said to you."

"Basically, she let me know that she isn't going nowhere."

"I told you she's jealous and conniving because I've moved on. The separation situation was not my fault. Her sickness made her paranoid and stressed. That caused her to have two miscarries that made her mental health worse. I tried to deal with it, but she wouldn't get the help she needed. I jumped into a relationship with her because I was hurt after you ghosted me. I love you, baby. Please, trust me she always knew I never stopped loving you. I will never do anything to hurt you. I'm gonna handle her."

"Okay, I'm going to trust that you're being honest with me. I will let you deal with her as you see fit, but this needs to be done and over with soon."

Feeling the anger release from her body, Endy allowed herself the pleasure of being in Rich's arms. She turned towards him and gently kissed his lips as his hands snaked around her waist. Feeling his hands on her body like that ignited a flame in Endy.

AFTER THE BETRAYAL

She deepened the kiss and felt his bulge respond in favor. Endy kneaded Rich's manhood from the outside of his pants, and from the low moan that he let out, she could tell he was just as much in the mood as she was.

"You sure you want me to fuck you with your parents in the house?" teased Rich.

"Yep. More than you will ever know."

Rich hoisted Endy up in the air and maneuvered them to the balcony wall. He had fucked her just about everywhere in the house, so it was time to get creative. They were going to fuck in the open air for anyone to watch—if they so happened to take a stroll in the backyard. Endy knew what Rich was doing, and her pussy moistened at the thought of being caught.

Rich slammed his lips onto Endy's and began to strip her clothes, kissing the area of exposed skin as each layer of clothing came off. Endy returned the favor by paying special attention to Rich's erection. Endy teased the tip a little before stuffing it into her mouth. She sucked in her jaws as she went deeper and swirled her tongue as she began bobbing her head. Rich would cum in no time if she kept the momentum going, and Endy so desperately wanted to make her man explode.

She began fondling his balls and alternating between sucking the tip and his balls. Rich was a withering mess under her, and she loved it. Rich wanted to nut inside Endy, so he stopped her from continuing and bent her up against the wall. Since he was taller than Endy, he had to squat a little, but that made no difference for him with the goal of sliding into her warm pussy with ease.

Seeing Endy's face smushed against the wall and her ass tooted in the air made him go primal. He wanted to go slow and enjoy Endy's body, but seeing her this way made him want to fuck her brains out. So, he did. He could tell Endy wasn't expecting that, but as much as he gave to her, she gave back twofold.

"Mmm, Rich. Mmm, damn, baby! Ah, baby," Endy loudly moaned, not caring if someone heard them.

He squatted lower and began to thrust against her G-spot. Endy's body shook at this new adjustment. He knew they wouldn't last long if they kept up this pace, but he didn't care. He wanted to thrust his dick into her–Endy's dick and only hers.

Endy's body tensed under his hand, and he knew she was about to cum. He bent her body upwards until she was flush against his chest. Then he angled her head a little to the side to suck on her neck. He continued to pound into her; as his balls tightened, he quickened his pace.

"Let's cum together, baby," he moaned.

Endy could only moan back in response. The amount of pleasure coursing through her body was unlike anything she had ever felt before. All too soon, it came to an end as Rich exploded inside her. Feeling his release made Endy's orgasm even more intense.

"Endy, I know y'all not being nasty right now!" Niema yelled through the door.

"Girl, we talking. I'm coming in a minute," Endy replied breathlessly.

Rich guided them to the bed, ignoring Niema's exclamations.

◆ ♥ ◆ Royalty Crowned ◆ ♥ ◆

After making Niema wait an hour, they finally got to Crabtree Valley Mall in Raleigh to shop. Endy was happy to get away from Rich's mother. Niema could tell something was wrong with Endy, but she couldn't put her finger on it. She knew Endy would eventually confide in her. Until then, she wanted to make sure Endy enjoyed herself.

"So, you have the mother-in-law from hell?" Niema laughed.

"Girl, a mess––an absolute mess, man. You see my father ain't no better." Endy shook her head.

"Girl, I was like how my friend deal," Niema said as she continued to laugh.

"But that's not it. You know Rich's ex-wife pulled up on me at the supermarket today, girl?"

"Wait! What?! Here? What did she say?"

"Nothing really. He did tell me she lost two children from him. She's bipolar and mentally ill girl. I have to be really careful."

"Well, don't let that bitch come between y'all. He's been showing and proving. If he isn't showing any signs otherwise, fuck her, Endy."

"Girl, I got a little heated. I'm going to let him handle it, though. If he doesn't, I told him I will."

"You know I'm here if you need me, Endy. Just keep your eyes and ears open, sis."

"Girl, you know me. That's a given. I'm not a slow leak. He knows that, too."

After a few hours of shopping, they decided to go home. Endy dreaded going back to deal with Patricia, but there was no escaping it. As they pulled into the yard, Niema jumped straight out of the car and put her bags in her car.

"Before we go in, are you sure you're good, sis?" Niema asked.

"Yes, girl! I'm fine. Tomorrow we can go to Best Buy for my TV. I'm gonna watch the rest of the football game and relax," Endy said as she opened the door.

The women joined their men as they watched the game, and Tanya, Aunt Sally, and Patricia listened to oldies and danced in the family room. Endy had the loft area of the house made up as a theater room. Niema saw how much Rich loved Endy and how attentive he was to her needs. She was excited that they both were finally in a happy place with their relationships.

A little after ten that evening, everyone gathered to leave. Thanksgiving for everyone was different that year, but they made the best out of it.

"You sure y'all don't want to take none of this food?" Endy asked Niema.

"No, girl. Aunt Sally cooked, too. Love y'all. I'll talk to you later." Niema hugged Endy as they prepared to head home.

"Okay, I'll walk y'all out so I can hit my blunt before I lay it down," Endy said.

She grabbed her purse and walked them outside to the car. After everyone left, she sat on the porch and sparked her blunt. She loved the relaxation she encountered in the South and wanted to enjoy her high before calling it a night.

When she was done and about to walk back into the house, she heard something in the bushes. Endy turned around quickly but didn't see anything. People warned her about the wildlife, so she ignored it. Right when she reached to twist the doorknob, a voice materialized.

"Hmm, I see Rich did well for himself this time," Maribel said, appearing out of nowhere.

"Bitch, what the fuck are you doing here? How the hell do you know where we live?" a startled Endy yelled as she pulled her .380 from her purse.

"Oh, you're a gutsy chica, huh?" Maribel laughed.

"Bitch, don't play with me. You're really crazy, aren't you? You got five seconds to get the fuck off my property before I blow your ass away!"

Endy cocked the gun.

"Honey, it's not that serious. I just want what I'm owed. If he wants to marry you and live happily ever after, I couldn't care less, but he needs to give me what I want!"

"Trick, your best bet is to get the fuck off my property now!"

"Or what? What you gon' do? You must not know who I am. I bet Jay and YaYa can tell you. Better yet, my sister, Nina, and cousin, Reeko, can tell you." Maribel laughed wickedly.

"What? Nina...your sister? Bitch, fuck you, Jay, and YaYa! Are y'all that damn bothered? You know, you're really delusional, honey. Please seek help. Rich told me all about your bipolar, schizophrenia, insecure, violent, sex-addicted ass. He's mine now, hoe! So, take your looney ass on. If you come one more step, I will use this gun on your trifling ass," Endy spat, placing her finger on the trigger.

AFTER THE BETRAYAL

"Girl, you let another bitch steal your man. He was so lost and confused without his Endy that I slipped right in and seduced his dumbass. How do you think YaYa knew where y'all anniversary was last year? Who do you think helped her plan that out so you could find them? Nina, your lawyer? That's my sister, you dumb bitch. Reeko? That's my first cousin! The Perez Family is my family, dumbass. I know everything there is to know about you, Ms. Endyia Hinton," Maribel said, chuckling.

"Lady, I don't know or even care what you're talking about. I'm telling you now; I will use this gun on your ass. I don't give a fuck who your family is. Your best bet is to get the hell on. Jay is responsible for his own actions. Now get your crazy ass on, bitch! Unless you want to die tonight!"

"Bitch, fuck you! You're like a fungus that won't go away. Me and Rich were happy. We were so happy. We were moving forward, but he just couldn't let you go—the so-called love of his life who left him crying. He's willing to let me go for your weak ass?" Maribel let out an evil laugh as tears streamed down her face.

Maribel charged at her, and before Endy knew it, she shot her twice—on the hip and the lower leg. The noise was so loud that everyone ran outside. Endy stood in her place, paralyzed and in shock. Everything happened so fast.

"What the hell is going on? Endyia, who is this woman?" Eddie yelled when he saw the woman on the ground bleeding.

"Who is this, Endy? What happened?" Tanya cried.

"Oh shit, baby! Are you okay? Did she hurt you?" Rich panicked, grabbing the gun out of her hands.

"Baby, who is this? Why did you shoot her, Endy? Baby, why?" Tanya cried.

"Rich's ex-wife," Endy sobbed.

"Rich, how the hell did this lunatic know where you live?" Patricia questioned.

"She must have followed me or gotten someone to locate Endy. Nothing is in my name. I'm so sorry, baby," Rich whimpered as he hugged Endy tightly, swaying her back and forth.

"The police are on the way! Oh, my goodness, she's bleeding a lot," Patricia yelled.

"How am I going to give you permission to marry my daughter if stuff like this is happening?" Eddie grilled Rich.

"Sir, I promise you this is not what it looks like. She has a mental disorder. We are divorced but have properties together. She's been in a relationship for the last two years, and I haven't had any problems until I started dating," Rich tried to explain.

"Baby, come on in. You're shaking like a leaf," Tanya told her daughter.

Twenty minutes later, the police and ambulance arrived. Endy already had proof of harassment when she assaulted her in her New York condo. Well, known in the Wake County area, Rich was already prepared to get lawyers and a judge involved.

The EMS took Maribel to Wake Medical Hospital, where she was treated and later released into police custody. The police advised the family to follow Endy to the station. They arrested her and took her downtown for a statement. They then filed a police report of the incident.

Endy was shaken up and exhausted, but she wasn't released until the next morning. She had to be back in court the next business day. Tanya felt she needed to be checked out, so they went to Duke Raleigh Hospital. All Endy wanted was to see her babies and go home.

When they all got back to the house, the family sat in the theater room and watched Martin reruns. Endy was extremely quiet, however, which worried everyone. Once every-one fell asleep, Endy went to the kitchen to get something to drink.

"Ma? Ma, are you good?" Rich asked her.

"Babe, I got something to tell you," Endy replied seriously.

"What's wrong?" Rich questioned; a bit nervous. He didn't want to lose her.

AFTER THE BETRAYAL

"You're gonna be a daddy. I'm two and a half months pregnant, Rich."

"Why are you crying? That's great news! I got you, ma! I promise...I got you," Rich replied enthusiastically and kissed her.

Epilogue
Six months Later

K.I.S.S.I.N.G by NAS

I t was the day of Endy and Rich's wedding; May 23, 2015. They chose to do the ceremony in Paris at a beautiful venue and flew the family out. They had their beautiful baby girl, who was born two months prematurely in March. They named her Promyse, and she looked just like Rich. Endy was worried that her early arrival would throw off the wedding, but Rich made sure his baby was happy. He loved Endy even more now that she had his first child.

The two of them had been in the happiest place since they got past that horrible incident from Thanksgiving night. Endy got five years' probation and ninety days house arrest. It was still better than her having to go to prison and deliver her baby there.

"Girl, how are you feeling? Are you nervous?" Chynna asked her.

"No, I'm actually ready to do it. I love him so much, y'all," Endy teared up.

"Bitch, don't start crying! We can't mess up our makeup," Ari grilled her.

"You deserve all of this," Niema told her. "You have been through so much hell. You kept us in good spirits when we were down. It's time we're there for you."

AFTER THE BETRAYAL

"Ny, you ain't never lied. We done worried the hell out of poor Endy," Ari added. "Friend, you have grown so much. I appreciate everything you have ever done for my kids and me."

"If you bitches don't want me to cry, y'all got to stop this," a choked-up Endy laughed.

"For real, though. I know we've all been through some shit, but you are the true definition of resilience and strength, Endy. I could have never dealt with a child Reeko had on me. I commend you on wanting Lil' Jay to grow up with the kids and treating him as your own. Then to know all them motherfuckers were in cahoots and played you—from YaYa to Nina to Jay. Girl, YaYa can't do anything but respect you for the woman you are," Chynna's voice trembled.

"Speaking of YaYa, she sends her love. You know she's constantly apologized for her actions. I just hope she uses this time away to fully rehabilitate herself. Hell, she and Maribel both because those two are very special cases. I never knew mental health could make people so devious, but I guess love makes you do crazy shit," Niema groaned.

"Maribel finally agreed and took the two million dollars she was offered for the properties. She went back to P.R. with her family so she could get the help she needed. Oh, and Nina tried to reach out to apologize, but I don't want to deal with her on any level. She put my family and me in jeopardy. There's no coming back from that," Endy expressed.

"I get it, honey. And to know she was Reeko's cousin the whole time. I see why she was in foster care. She probably was hell on wheels," Chynna laughed.

"I mean, for real, though," Ari added.

Endy stood up to look in the mirror. Her dress was stunning. It was a mermaid lace wedding dress with the backless part showing off her tattoo. Her shoes were made like glass slippers, and the headpiece consisted of genuine diamonds that encircled her head. She teared up just looking at herself, knowing all she had encountered in the last couple of years.

"Baby girl, you ready?" Eddie's voice snapped her out of her trance.

Endy smiled. "Yes, I am, Daddy."

The décor was elegant. They didn't want a wedding party, but they did ask everyone to wear white. The song All of Me by John Legend started to play. The best part of it all was that John Legend himself was there to sing. Endy didn't realize it until she started walking down the aisle and saw him to her left on the piano. The tears immediately dropped; she couldn't help herself.

As she got closer to her husband-to-be, she saw he was also in tears. Rich always dreamed of the day when he would make her his wife—and it finally came true.

Endy had finally got her happily ever after. Even though she knew the future wouldn't be perfect, she found peace in knowing that she had a faithful and committed man for her and their children. The road had always been rough for Endy, but she prevailed in the end despite it all.

Endy's marketing company, The Come-Up Media, was doing well. The kids were all situated in daycare, and the stores were doing monetarily great. Karishma released her clothing line and sold out within a few days. Things were finally going good for Endy, and she made sure her family was good, too. Eddie decided to move him and his wife to North Carolina to help Endy out with the kids since he was retired. It seemed like, for once, everything was falling into place for Endy.

Meanwhile, YaYa got sentenced to twelve years in prison for kidnapping, communicating a threat, and discharging fire arm in public. Jasean got forty years in the feds for conspiracy to murder, racketeering, money laundering, and extortion. Caine, who was on the run, went down to Florida with some family. Marilyn and Evelyn opened up a nursing home and home health agency in Queens. Keosha found her happy ending and moved with Juwan from New York to Pennsylvania. She wanted to raise Cadence in a safer environment. They were also at Endy and Rich's wedding. Finally, everyone had moved on with their

AFTER THE BETRAYAL

lives and lived life accordingly.

How can one be faithful in life when one can't commit to change? There is still life after the betrayal.